Smiling, Kipp Halstead pulled off my ~~hair~~ net. "A strawberry blond," he said with satisfaction. "Now let's see if you have passion worth taking."

"No," I protested, turning my mouth away. But one large hand cupped my chin and brought it around.

Using the steely strength of his other hand, he pressed me to him, my breasts against his chest, my thighs against his. Then his lips consumed my mouth.

Panic and anger were lost in that instant. My body was caught in a devil's wind, vulnerable and naked to the message of his lips and tongue.

He buried his mouth near my ear and tugged it lightly with his lips. Then he released me slowly. "Had enough for your first lesson?" How could I say yes—when my senses screamed for more. . . ?

SWEEPING PASSIONS

☐ **THE SECOND SISTER by Leslie O'Grady.** Winner of the *Romantic Times'* Best Historical Gothic Award. Beautiful Cassandra Clark was an innocent when she arrived at the elegant Victorian mansion of the mother she never knew. But her innocence was soon shattered when she learned the true meaning of desire in the forbidden arms of the brooding, domineering man who was her half-sister's husband. "Titillating suspense!"—*Romantic Times*   (146476—$2.95)

☐ **AFTER THE TORCHLIGHT by Diane Carey.** It was fear at first sight when the beautiful Jean Forbes entered the menacing castle of her distant cousin, Gregory—and passion at first touch when she gave herself to him. But even as she surrendered to the power of her growing desire, dark secrets threatened to envelope the handsome, brooding man she was so desperate to love.   (145615—$2.95)

☐ **HAREM by Diane Carey.** Jessica Grey watched ruggedly handsome Tarik Pasha crossing the moonlit floor. This was her captor ... the rebel leader who kidnapped her and gave her away to the Sultan's harem where women were taught the art of making love. It was here that Jessica learned the deepest secrets of passion—secrets that could truly make her desire's slave....   (143353—$3.95)

☐ **UNDER THE WILD MOON by Diane Carey.** Katie was Will Scarlet's prisoner, yet she moaned with pleasure as his gentle touch made her forget that he was one of Robin Hood's bandits. For although he had taken her by force, he was keeping her, now, by love. Tonight a deep primeval rhythm would unite them so that no sword, no prince, could part them—now or forever....   (141547—$3.95)

☐ **WINTER MASQUERADE by Kathleen Maxwell.** Lovely Kimberly Barrow was enthralled by the glorious winter splendor of William and Mary's court and the two devastatingly attractive men vying for her attentions. But her hidden secret thrust her into a dangerous game of desire....   (129547—$2.95)

Prices slightly higher in Canada.

Beware, My Love

Lee Karr

A SIGNET BOOK

NEW AMERICAN LIBRARY

PUBLISHER'S NOTE

This novel is a work of fiction. Names, characters, places, and incidents either are the product of the author's imagination or are used fictitiously, and any resemblance to actual persons, living or dead, events, or locales is entirely coincidental.

NAL BOOKS ARE AVAILABLE AT QUANTITY DISCOUNTS WHEN USED TO PROMOTE PRODUCTS OR SERVICES. FOR INFORMATION PLEASE WRITE TO PREMIUM MARKETING DIVISION, NEW AMERICAN LIBRARY, 1633 BROADWAY, NEW YORK, NEW YORK 10019.

Copyright © 1987 by Leona Karr

SIGNET TRADEMARK REG. U.S. PAT. OFF. AND FOREIGN COUNTRIES
REGISTERED TRADEMARK—MARCA REGISTRADA
HECHO EN CHICAGO, U.S.A.

SIGNET, SIGNET CLASSIC, MENTOR, ONYX, PLUME, MERIDIAN and NAL BOOKS are published by New American Library, 1633 Broadway, New York, New York 10019

First Printing, March, 1987

1 2 3 4 5 6 7 8 9

PRINTED IN THE UNITED STATES OF AMERICA

To Natalie C. Warner,
In sun and shade, my dear friend

1

I knocked again. "Hello . . . Is anybody there?"

My voice sounded thin and ridiculous as it swept away into the vastness of brooding lodge-pole pines, vaulting ponderosas, and scraggly Engelmann spruce crowding the building. Standing in the dark shadows of the long, narrow hotel veranda, I strained to hear any response behind the locked, heavy-planked door. Only a faint crackling mocked me . . . logs settling in their notched cradles? Or had someone shifted weight somewhere inside the cavernous structure?

I know it's the right place, I thought. In the dusk of late afternoon, the jagged silhouette of craggy mountains brought a wild beating of my pulse into my throat. Like angry wings, needled branches whipped all around me. I shivered as banks of chilled air swept through them and made a high-pitched moaning. With panic racing through my veins like the onset of a fever, I lifted the folds of my teal-blue traveling dress and starched petticoats, stepped off the porch, and raised my eyes to check again the painted sign that read, "The Lacey Hotel."

My gaze flickered over the steep mansard roof, attic dormer windows, gingerbread eaves, white clapboard exterior, and stained-glass doors which gave the building a hint of Victorian elegance. My aunt and uncle had written proudly of their hotel, and even after Uncle Benjamin's death a year ago, Aunt Esther had continued to write me about improvements she was making. Remembering what she had written to me in her last letter about this hotel, which now lay ghostly silent, sent my thoughts and fears in a frantic whirling.

"The only thing I have left is the hotel . . . and now evil forces are trying to take it from me," she had written to me at Miss Purcell's Academy for Young Ladies, where I taught. I saw with alarm that her writing had deteriorated into frantic scrawls, and the cryptic note was filled with dire declarations: "There's no one I can trust . . . I fear for my very life . . . please come . . . you are my only hope." Only the lack of money and my obligations as schoolmistress kept me from running off at a moment's notice to the rugged gold mining town located in the high country west of Denver. Now my laggardly arrival three months later taunted me. I should have come sooner.

Bare windows stared back at me like blind eyes, clouded and opaque . . . lifeless. A hushed foreboding warning emanated from the building, alerting my instincts. Like a faint odor, the sensation of danger touched my nostrils and then disappeared before recognition could capture it. I took a step backward as if the brooding silence were alive and pushing me away. For a long moment I stared at the locked double door and blank hotel windows like one mesmerized by disbelief . . . stilling an impulse to run away as fast as I could. Then I took myself in hand and sat down on the edge of a step to collect my thoughts. I was exhausted and near tears. What should I do now? Had I come too late?

During the long train ride across the Kansas and Colorado prairies in a jolting Union Pacific passenger car, I had clung to my stubborn conviction that I was doing the right thing by making the journey. Miss Purcell had warned me that a gold-mining town was no place for a twenty-year-old girl who'd been raised on a Kansas farm. She was appalled that I would even consider going into such uncivilized territory—and alone! Men would notice me, she warned, eyeing my reddish-blond hair with a rueful expression and pursing her mouth at my full bust, which even a high-necked, starched muslin bodice could not disguise. She had filled my ears wtih tales of greedy prospectors, unscrupulous businessmen, overnight millionaires, and fancy ladies who drank and swore and gave themselves to a man for a dollar. Her warnings had not deterred me but were like the tempting voice of the Lorelei. Although I didn't admit it even to myself, I felt that once I reached my next birthday of twenty-one, I would have joined the ranks of irreversible spinsterhood. Life would never change for me then. Year after year, my charges would seem younger and younger and my joy would come from vicariously watching them marry and have children . . . whom, in time, I would teach. I felt desperately alone . . . without family and close kin . . . and life was marching away from my youth. Even if Aunt Esther had not been as dear to me as my own departed mother, I would have answered the summons that brought a feeling of excitement and change into my life.

The train had been dusty, and crowded, and dimly lit with candles swinging in glass globes at each end of the fifty-foot passenger cars. A large stove gave out smoke and heated the close, odoriferous air. Despite the uncomfortable accommodations, I had been grateful that the transcontinental railroad had been completed a year before so I didn't have to cross miles and miles of unrelieved terrain by stagecoach. No one took notice of me except a large gray-haired woman who shared my seat. "Aren't you a pretty one?" she cackled. "You'll turn the fellows' heads, I'll wager, with that amber-red hair and eyes the color of warm honey." I blushed at her breezy compliments and felt more conspicuous than ever. Mrs. Berry told me she was going to visit her son in Manitou Springs, Colorado—"The hot waters there will be good for my lumbago" —and proceeded to tell me about her numerous ailments. A friendly soul, she bought food for both of us from vendors at various stations along the way. While she slept, I sat for hours looking out the window, with a new novel, *Lorne Doone*, lying unopened in my lap.

As the barren landscape swept by, occasionally I saw an abandoned sod hut in the distance where someone had tried to make a home and failed. As far as the eye could see, buffalo grass stretched to the horizon like waves of a yellow-green sea. The land was a sharp contrast to the patchwork of cultivated fields around my home in Hartford, Kansas. As the train moved across eastern Colorado, I felt as if I were leaving civilization behind for a raw, untamed country which Miss Purcell had warned me could defeat the strongest of men and women. Her stories about whole families who had perished trying to cross the great Continental Divide settled uneasily upon me.

When the Rocky Mountains appeared as a line of jagged peaks pasted against a translucent pearl-blue sky, apprehension sent a cold prickling of sweat upon my weary body. How could I ever find my way in such stark, majestic mountains? They intensified my feeling of smallness . . . of inadequacy . . . and instilled doubts about my own ability to survive in such a remote region. Uncle Benjamin had been killed in a fall . . . his body found at the bottom of a ravine . . . and now Aunt Esther feared for her life. Why did I think I would escape such violence?

At Denver City I changed trains and boarded a tiny passenger car of a narrow-gauge railroad line. I was sorry to say good-bye to Mrs. Berry, and as the car filled up, I tried to keep my eyes downcast and still peer at the new arrivals as they passed by my seat. Almost all of them

11

were men, roughly dressed and bewhiskered. Only two women came aboard. I hoped they would sit near me, but they passed my seat without a glance.

A whiff of musk perfume touched my nostrils as one of them passed. She wore a fashionable plumed velvet bonnet but her face was swathed in a heavy veil and I couldn't see whether she was young or old. Her gown was a willow green trimmed with velvet rouleau and her waist-length cape was lined with satin. Both garments seemed rather worn. Her closed parasol was the same shade of pale green as her dress. I noticed that one of her green cloth gloves had a slight rip in the thumb. I could not but wonder about her.

The other girl, a dark brunette with a rather plump figure, managed a portmanteau and hat-box. She was dressed in a cambric gown that had seen better days, making me wonder if she was a companion or servant to the mystery lady. I don't know why I thought of her that way—my romantic tendencies, I suppose. Miss Purcell was always chiding me about my imagination. Mystery lady, indeed—but I could not help but wonder why the woman was so heavily veiled and why she was going to Glen Eyrie. After Mrs. Berry's open friendliness, I felt more alone than ever.

I opened my book but my gaze fell unseeing on Mr. Blackmore's new novel. Miss Purcell had given it to me to help pass the long journey, but a fluttering anxiety would not let me concentrate on the words. Two men sitting across the aisle from me looked at me boldly. Their frank looks were impolite and suggestive. A bawdy exchange between the two of them about strawberry blonds brought color into my cheeks. I kept my back rigid with as haughty a demeanor as I could assume. My hands gripped the chain on my beaded reticule and felt sweaty under my chamois gloves. Every rumbling grind of the train wheels seemed to take me toward a disaster promised by the treacherous cliffs and craggy slopes that were now outside my window.

The tracks curved so that I could peer ahead and see our sooty, puffing locomotive as it chugged and twisted along sheer precipices. At times the train clung precariously to rocky shelves no wider than the railroad track. One faulty move and . . . ! I closed my eyes, fighting against a sensation of plunging off into that chasm. Heights always bothered me and I felt a paralyzing vertigo as I looked down at rushing white waters deep in the canyon.

For hours our laboring, tiny engine groaned its way over rugged passes like a belching iron monster in labor and inched the rocking train cars upward until at last we reached the high mountain town, Glen Eyrie—Valley of Eagles. Well-named, I had thought as I peered out of the window at a tiny, crude town caught in the bottom of a gulch. Although it was the first of June, there were few signs of spring in this high country. I craned my neck to see mountains soaring up on every side and rolling wooded slopes of dark green conifers. The sun had already dropped behind a range of jagged

13

peaks and the first wash of gray twilight blanketed the valley as the train groaned to a stop.

Collecting my reticule and shawl, I stepped off the train. I must have looked indecisive, for the two rude men alighted after me and exchanged remarks about "the little lady needing help." One of them took a swaggering step toward me. Using my schoolmarm demeanor, which could control a classroom full of obstreperous students, I gave him a look that withered him in his tracks and swept past him.

I allowed myself a silent smile as I entered the station and made arrangements to pick up my small trunk and portmanteau later. I knew my aunt's hotel was not far from the station and the walk would feel good after the inactivity of my long journey. When I came out after talking to the stationmaster, I was relieved to see the two aggressive men had gone on their way. The mystery lady and her companion were still on the platform, apparently waiting for some baggage to be unloaded, and I passed without either of them looking in my direction.

I followed a rough board sidewalk toward the main intersection of King and Pearl streets. I found both names to be complete misnomers: there was nothing royal or precious about the false-fronted buildings built of timber hastily cut from the nearby hillsides. The only structures that looked permanent were a bank building and jail of gray stone. The streets were bordered by unpainted structures with crude signs identifying businesses like Jerry's Mercantile Store, Golddust Newspaper, and Hawkins' Livery Stable, where the sounds of a blacksmith's anvil vibrated through open doors. Whiskered men lounging outside a saloon leered at me as I passed, grinning lewdly as they deftly spit tobacco on the boardwalks.

I pulled my shawl tighter as a cold ripple went up my spine. The sun had barely set and a boisterous nightlife was obviously gearing up in the gambling halls and saloons. It would not be safe to wander the streets alone much longer. I knew that it would take more than a haughty demeanor to keep me out of harm in the shadows of this frontier town.

Dusty lanterns were already being lighted along narrow streets, which were cut into the steep slopes on both sides of the gulch. My eyes followed long spans of wooden stairs which led from one level to the next, where small, crude houses had been built almost on top of each other. Tiny front porches on the houses seemed to hang out precariously over empty air, and I saw with a start that some of the outhouses were two-story, in case snow closed off the bottom one. It seemed to me that only rough rock walls kept the whole of Glen Eyrie from sliding down into the gulch and creek. The whole town had been built in a higgledy-piggledy fashion, like a ragamuffin outgrowing the seams of his patched clothes. I coughed and covered my nose as an ore wagon drawn by a six-horse team rumbled by.

How anxious I was to gain the sanctuary of the Lacey Hotel and feel the welcoming arms of my aunt around my weary shoulders! When I reached the third block on Pearl Street, I hurried toward the sign for the hotel. Even before I reached the building, I knew something was wrong. My stomach lurched. It couldn't be. Where was the bustle of life, the noise and activity that I had expected? I knocked on the door and called out, but no one answered.

No . . . no . . . it couldn't be! My hands tightened in my chamois gloves and I sat on the steps and struggled to contain my disappointment and rising anxiety. Surely someone would have sent me word if Aunt Esther had died. Besides, the hotel looked as if it had been shut up for some time. Its deserted air hinted of months of closure. The wooden floor of the narrow veranda was dusty, and all the front windows were clouded and unwashed. Eerie silence in front of the hotel testified that wagons and buggies had not recently disgorged any boarders at its doors.

And yet I had received a letter in recent months. Perhaps Aunt Esther had closed the hotel and was living in quarters in the back. A surge of relief brought new energy. I stood up, brushed off the dust from my draped skirt of blue levantine, and quickly made my way around the corner of the building, intent upon pursuing this line of reasoning. Indecision was not one of my failings; in fact, I often lunged forward into a hasty action that I later regretted, simply because I was too often impatient, enthusiastic, or boldly direct in my approach. Miss Purcell had often admonished me that "looking before leaping" was a wise adage which had stood the test of time. More than once my temper had flared in unladylike conduct, resulting in rash action which I later regretted. However, if impulsiveness was one unfortunate trait in my character, stubbornness was another. Consequently, it never crossed my mind to turn to someone for help or enlightenment in the situation.

It was getting dark. The path around the building was snarled and overgrown, verifying its disuse. Pine needles and wild mountain grass, moist from an earlier rain, sank under the heels of my button shoes and soiled the edges of my skirt and petticoats with moist red dirt. Decaying leaves, damp earth, rotting wood, and the ever-present spicy scent of pine assaulted my nostrils with a pungent incense. Somewhere beyond the infinity of evergreen trees was the muted, relentless roar of a stream.

If I hadn't found another door halfway along the side of the building, I might have turned back. The hope that I would find my aunt, hale and hearty, inside made me turn a blackened brass knob and then breathe a sigh of relief as it creaked open. I peered in, hesitating for a moment before entering its shadowy interior. "Aunt Esther . . . Aunt Esther . . ." My voice sounded frail and hollow as it echoed into the shadowy cavern.

I firmed my chin and went in. For a moment my eyes refused to focus in the dim light coming through the two tall, narrow windows flanking the door. When my pupils had dilated enough, I found myself in a small entry. As I moved forward through an archway, fine dust rose in clouds under my footsteps and filtered into my nose and mouth. The only sound I heard was the wild thumping of my heart as I penetrated the shadowy interior of the building. A long room stretched to the front door— the lobby, I determined, for in the dim light I could see a reception counter along one side and a long flight of stairs in the center leading upward. A narrow hall ran to the back of the building.

"Hello . . . is anybody here?" My voice bounded upward into the darkness as I paused at the foot of the stairs and looked up. Dank smells and musty odors drifted down to me. In the waiting silence, the overpowering presentiment that I was not alone was undeniable . . . as if I had intruded upon some unseen drama. I swung around with my eyes rounded, searching the depths of the room, where clusters of chairs and tables were shoved together in cluttered masses. A silent piano stood in the corner. There had not been laughter or talking in this room for a long time, and yet my ears filled with cheering, clapping, and the frantic chords of impelling music. A cry broke from my throat, shattering the brooding silence of the empty lobby.

Then I froze!

I heard the sound of a door opening.

In the darkness at the end of the long corridor running to the back of the building, I saw lamplight suddenly spill out into the hall. My first thought was that I had been right. My aunt was living in quarters at the rear of the hotel! With my usual impulsiveness, I bounded forward, only to halt with a startled gasp as I reached the open door.

I saw him then, within the radius of the lamplight. For a suspended moment his powerful torso and stance exuded the same overpowering sensation as the granite Rocky Mountains outside the weathered building. I had been terrified by their awesome power and threatening force. I trembled with that same feeling now.

Even though shock had tightened my throat, I never once considered bolting. As he moved purposefully forward, I saw something flash in his hand. For one terrifying instant I thought it was a sword or dueling pistol . . . but with relief realized it was only a cane fashioned with a silver top and tip. "Who are you?" I managed, barely.

"I might ask you the same thing." His voice mocked. Through the open door, a wash of lamplight fell upon his face and I saw that his penetrating gray-blue eyes held the hint of storm clouds in their depths, promising fury like forked lightning if his anger were aroused. He was in his thirties, his features handsomely craggy; a wide-bridged nose which might have been broken once or twice separated his bold eyes, and devil-black eyebrows flared thickly above them; large, nicely curved lips gave him a sensitive and at the same time a cruel, hard look. He looked at me with a devilish, sensual expression and in that intuitive second I knew that I must turn and flee.

But as I turned, he swiftly locked his cane behind me, with his hands securing it against the small of my back. In an instant the cane was like an iron rod holding me prisoner.

"Intruders must answer for their actions," he taunted, his tone at once half-threatening, half-teasing.

A pool of light in the dark hall engulfed us in an eerie intimacy. My heart lurched about with a frantic beat. "Then . . . then I suggest you begin, sir," I managed in my schoolmistress tone, much too aware of how close his body was to mine.

He raised a devilish eyebrow. "Indeed? And by what great leap did you arrive at the conclusion that I am the intruder?"

"Because your manner is beyond rudeness and presumption!" As he held the cane across my back, I felt caught in his embrace, close enough to be aware of every breath he drew.

"Come now. Let me welcome you to Glen Eyrie. I heard that Millie was expecting a new boarder. Apparently you took the wrong turn at King Street. Her place is in the opposite direction." He chuckled. "My good fortune. She wouldn't mind if I tasted the wares before anybody else." He pulled me closer until the buttons of my bodice brushed against his waistcoat. Instinctively I pushed forcibly against him, but the feel of the sinewy, hard chest only gave me a sense of the physical vitality and strength under his soft cambric shirt. Unwillingly my hips were pressed against legs encased in smooth-fitting nankeen trousers tucked in high boots.

The spicy, outdoor scent of his masculinity caused a moment of vertigo.

"No . . ." I closed my eyes and tried to jerk away.

He laughed. "How charming . . . but your little games are not necessary. I'm willing to add the first gold coin to your earnings."

"I . . . I am not what you think!" I gasped, my head reeling from this domination of my senses. "I suggest you cease this barbaric behavior . . ." His lips came dangerously near mine.

"And if I don't?"

"Then I will have to summon someone in authority." My voice was pitifully weak.

He threw back his head and laughed. "It's obvious you haven't been in Glen Eyrie for more than a few minutes. If you had, you wouldn't make such a meaningless threat." He tightened his grip on the cane, pulling me forward. He bent his head to mine as his chest pressed against my breasts, and I wondered if he knew the sudden fire that burst from the contact. He grinned. "May I introduce myself? Kipp Halstead, Esquire, who, in his not-so-modest way, runs this town!"

"And everybody in it, I suppose," I countered angrily. An aura of domination was in every breath he drew. Was he the evil my aunt had written me about? Fear made me gasp, "What have you done with my aunt?"

I felt him stiffen. "Aunt?" His eyebrows met over the bridge of his nose.

"I'm Allison Lacey. Aunt Esther wrote me . . . asking me to come."

21

At any other time I might have enjoyed his consternation. "You're Esther's niece?"

"If she's my aunt, then that's the correct relationship," I answered haughtily. He quickly removed his cane. I stepped back, glaring at him and trying to recover some degree of poise.

His laugh was shallow. "Please accept my apology. It seems that I am guilty of a social error."

I found his tone superior and infuriating. "I am not interested in your apology. I would appreciate it if you would tell me where I may find my aunt."

"Gladly. Suppose we find a more comfortable place for our conversation." Before I could protest, he had cupped my elbow in a firm grip and urged me forward through the doorway into a room that was well-lighted and fully furnished. Its contrast with the rest of the shadowy, dusty hotel was startling.

Who was this man—and what had he done with my aunt?

2

*T*HE room seemed to be an office of sorts; a handsome English desk with marble knobs on a myriad of pigeonholed drawers was covered with papers, maps, and books. An open inkwell and a freshly dipped pen told me he must have been writing when my presence had called him into the hall. A fire had already been lit against the evening chill in a stone fireplace. In front of the crackling logs stood two American-styled easy chairs with a small gate-leg table between them. It was also loaded down with books, charts, and what seemed to be rolled-up maps. Several crystal lamps glowed brightly near the desk and chairs. There was no mistaking a pistol lying on the desk in the midst of the clutter. My bewilderment was submerged by a growing sense of unreality. There was a nightmarish quality about the scene that made the back of my neck prickle. Something was wrong . . . terribly wrong.

"And now, Miss Lacey, please be seated," he drawled, "and we can—"

I interrupted him. "What have you done with my aunt?" I managed to keep my gaze locked on his infuriating half-grin.

"Done with her? Meaning, of course, what foul deeds have I perpetrated upon the dear lady?" He seemed amused, but I sensed that he was not all that comfortable with my appearance. "Please sit down. You must be weary from your journey. May I offer you—"

"Information. I am concerned about my aunt's whereabouts." I took a deep breath to steady myself. "You're correct, I am tired. Please answer my questions. I've come a long way . . . I'm very worried . . . I dislike unpleasantness."

Amused, he raised one eyebrow. I was certain that he was not used to having his company considered unpleasant. In the full light I saw that he was in his early thirties, over six feet tall, with massive shoulders and a tapered waist that verified well-toned muscles. Rich black hair curled on his neck and at his sideburns. He was now twirling the cane casually in his hand and I suspected that he carried it only as an accessory, not as an aid to any physical weakness. It had probably cracked more than one man's skull, and I felt myself paling at the thought. I was intensely relieved when his glower faded and he chuckled. "It seems that my charm has failed . . . for the moment. Please sit down and—"

"Where is my aunt, Mr. Halstead?"

He shrugged. "The lady is demanding an answer, I see." His dark eyes flashed.

He was going to drag out this meeting. Admitting defeat had never come easily for me, but I knew that I had no choice. With as much poise as I could manage, I walked over to one of the brocade chairs and sat down.

Grinning, he had the bad manners to remark, "Changed your mind, I see. Well, now, I happen to have a small bottle of spirits in my desk . . . if you would care to join me."

"No," I said through forced lips. Damn him!

"Unfortunately, I have only brandy."

"No, thank you."

"Oh, come now. A few sips will help revive you from the journey." He proceeded to take a bottle and two glasses out of his desk as if I had graciously accepted his hospitality.

I could feel color rising in my cheeks as he handed me a small glass filled with golden liquid that shimmered in the light. What good would it have done to admit that only once a year, at Christmastime, did I have sherry with Miss Purcell and the rest of the staff? I took the brandy but decided only to feign sipping it until I found out about my aunt.

"To Esther," he toasted with a click on my glass, and watched me put the glass to my lips before he sat down in the other chair. "May her health improve."

I caught my breath. "She's ill?"

A flicker of unexpected concern showed for a moment in his eyes. "I'm afraid she's . . . she's met with an accident."

I fear for my life! The frantic scrawl of my aunt's writing rose like a firebrand in my mind's eye. "An accident?"

25

"She was found unconscious behind the registration desk in the lobby. She must have fainted and fallen," he said smoothly, but his eyes narrowed just enough that I knew he was picking his words carefully. "Her skull was fractured . . . and she suffered a severe concussion."

The frantic tone of the letters came back. Aunt Esther had been afraid—but of what . . . or whom? Had she really fallen—or been attacked? Was it possible this powerful man had been responsible? Fear leapt within me at the unspoken question.

"We thought for a while Esther wasn't going to make it . . . but she's a fighter, your aunt," he said smoothly.

"And . . . and she's getting well?" I swallowed to control a sudden trembling.

He didn't answer directly. "I didn't know Esther had written to you."

And you're not pleased! The terror that had been in my aunt's scribbled writing now seemed very real, hovering in the air and closing in about me. By coming, had I pulled the cloak of evil over my own shoulders? I shoved the thought away. "My aunt and I are very close. She wrote me not once, but several times. I wanted to come immediately, but I couldn't. You see, I teach French and English in a school for young ladies . . ." For some reason it was important that he understand my delay in coming.

"And where is this school?"

"Hartford, Kansas."

He nodded. "I believe I remember Esther mentioning that she was from there."

"She is my mother's sister . . . a case of brothers marrying sisters," I explained. The "pretend" sips of brandy were relaxing me as the level of the warm liquid went down with my nervous sipping. "You see, Aunt Esther is really like my own mother. I lived with her and Uncle Benjamin in Hartford because our farm was a considerable distance from any school. When they decided to come to Colorado, I begged them to bring me with them . . . but, of course, they couldn't. They said a gold-mining camp was no place for a young girl. I returned to the farm because my own parents had need of me until their death a few years ago. After completing two years of study at a normal school, I secured my position at Miss Purcell's school. Up until Uncle Benjamin's death, all of Aunt Esther's letters had contained glowing accounts of the new improvements they were making in the hotel . . . a bigger kitchen and dining room . . . even the addition of a wine cellar . . ."

"Yes, the Lacey Hotel was getting the reputation of serving elegant cuisine and of being *the* place to stay," he agreed. I could not read his eyes. His voice was subtly edged with an emotion I could not identify.

"Until about six months ago, when these frantic letters started coming, I thought Aunt Esther was well and happy . . . and determined to carry out all the plans they had made."

"A proud woman, Esther—must run in the family," he said over the rim of his glass, those wintry eyes suddenly warm.

"But I don't understand. Where is she? How

27

long has the hotel been closed?" He was treating me like a captured mouse, feeding me one crumb at a time. He didn't know that my patience had a short fuse, and he was stretching it to its length. "I demand you tell me what horrible things have been happening to my aunt!"

"Demand?" His tone was taunting.

"Please . . ." I managed.

"Your aunt hung on as long as she could after your uncle's death, but in the end had to sell—to me."

I stiffened, clutching the half-full glass of brandy. Suddenly there was no warmth from either the fire or the fiery liquid that I'd been sipping. My poor aunt's words were as chilled as if they had been scrawled on a frosted windowpane: *The hotel is the only thing I have left— and evil forces are trying to take it from me.*

I turned and looked at his contemptible, satisfied smile. Fury exploded in my head like a red flare. I flung the remaining contents of my glass right into his face and a second later stood back and regarded what I'd done. Brandy dripped off his nose, into his astonished mouth, and down his chin. His expression would have made me laugh except that it had changed to one of black anger. The pure idiocy of my behavior struck me. "I'm sorry," I stammered, but it was much too late.

"You little . . ." He wiped the brandy with a swipe of one hand and jerked me to my feet with the other. "You had me fooled. I thought you were a lady." With that he jerked off my bonnet. "A strawberry blond," he said with satisfaction, "with a fiery temper to match. Now, let's see if you have passion worth the taking."

"No!" I pressed surprisingly strong hands against his chest and turned my mouth away. I was too late, as one large, smooth hand cupped my rebellious chin and brought it around.

I struggled, but his demanding, commanding fingers slipped to my throat and held me captive. My breath was nearly cut off, and my heart raced wildly. Using the steely strength of his other hand, he pressed me to him, crushing my breasts against his chest and trapping my thighs against his. Next, his lips pushed open my mouth.

Panic and anger were lost in that instant. My body felt caught in a devil's wind. I was vaguely aware that his hand had slipped away, allowing my breath to come more easily as he wrapped some of my loosened hair in his fist. His passion and strength seemed to penetrate the numerous folds of my dress and undergarments, leaving my slender body vulnerable and naked to the message of his lips and tongue. Desire, something new and forbidden, despite his roughness, possessed me. I was no longer passive in his embrace. My sudden response must have shocked him, and in that instant while he was off guard, I caught myself—with only my instinct for self-respect and survival still intact.

"Let me go." My voice was choked and tremulous.

His hands slipped to my waist, spanning my slender middle, and then his fingers rose to cup my swelling breasts. A bewildering tautness forced rosy buds to rub against the soft fold of my camisole. I knew the reaction had not escaped his notice.

"Please . . . let me go," I said before he could respond again—his passion aroused my innocent yet savage response.

He buried his mouth near my ear and tugged it lightly with his lips. Then he released me slowly. "Had enough for your first lesson?" he whispered as he tasted my flesh.

"First and last!" I managed.

He laughed lightly. "I think not." Now, more gently: "Put your bonnet back on . . . and I'll take you to see your aunt."

Releasing me, he went back to his desk and picked up his jacket that was tossed on a nearby chair. I stared at him, riveted to the spot where he left me. My body, so quickly and shockingly aroused, depleted of the strength, needed time to deal with this impossible male. Mesmerized, I glared at his bold profile, and the urge to fly at him with clawed fingernails disappeared. Instead I took a deep breath and jutted out my chin. It was true he had taught me one lesson—this aggressive male would take what he wanted! By some treachery, he had already taken the precious hotel from my beloved aunt. While it appeared to be too late to do anything about that, I knew that every man, even the arrogant Kipp Halstead, had his Achilles' heel . . . and with my usual stubborn willfulness, I intended to find it. Then I shuddered as a impossible thought hit me.

Maybe he had already found mine!

3

WE walked in almost total silence to the livery stable a short distance below the hotel. He kept one hand under my elbow and swung his cane jauntily in the other as if this were a casual early-evening stroll. His English-style riding jacket and tight-fitting nankeen trousers exaggerated his natural breadth of shoulders and muscular thighs. The sensual force that had exploded between us in the hotel lingered in the soft light as we walked together. My sudden vulnerability frightened me more than the presence of one Kipp Halstead, whom I did not trust, know, or understand! I needed all my wits about me. He could well be the evil my dear aunt had written about. His charm and passion could well be the devil's tool. It must be the brandy, I thought, cursing myself for being such a fool to accept a drink from so sensuous a villain. I had heard of men who plied women with liquor in order to have their way with them. I drew in deep breaths of chilled thin air and forced myself to walk rigidly beside him, my arm now stiff under his touch.

The western horizon held the last gray light of dusk and soon night would slide down the wooded slopes into the narrow mountain valley where eagles nested. I couldn't help but wonder what he was thinking about me. Had he been surprised by the burst of passion between us? Something in his manner indicated that he regretted having moved so fast . . . that he should have been more cautious . . . that like myself he was trying to recover from the intimacy that had engulfed us. I caught his speculative glance on me and his eyes were strangely somber and void of any teasing. I wondered how much of his light, debonair air was only a facade. What scars and hurts did Kipp Halstead, Esquire, hide from the world?

Politely he helped me into a smart black buggy, nicely swung, with tufted soft seats and gray upholstery. "We'll pick up your things at the station," he said in a conversational tone. "And then I'll take you to my house—"

My eyes widened. "Your house! You promised to take me to—"

"To Esther. But that's where she is. Does the prospect of being under my roof frighten you?" he challenged, and his smile said: Of course it does.

"No," I lied, determined that he wouldn't know how the thought sent peculiar shivers up my spine. I sat stiffly beside him on the tufted leather seat as he flicked a whip over a sleek, fast-moving gray mare. He maneuvered the buggy around horses, mules, wagons, and drays raising dust in the rutted streets. I was glad I was not out on the crowded streets alone, and yet any sense of feeling safe with this man was a mockery. What did I know about him except that he had taken Aunt Esther's hotel—and that his kisses seared like fire? Why was Aunt Esther in his house? To be a prisoner—*to die?*

The thought was too much to bear. It was obvious that he had not expected any of Esther's kin to arrive. What villainous plans had gone awry now that I was on the scene? How could I be certain that I wouldn't meet with an "accident" myself? I was positive that my aunt hadn't fallen, but had been struck hard enough to crack her skull and left on the floor of the hotel. It seemed to fit in with the fear and terror evident in her letters. There were questions that I was determined to answer—despite the complication of one Kipp Halstead!

Maybe it was the shadow of mountains that made everything look so bleak and gray . . . and alien. Stark granite cliffs absorbed the dark colors of night. Deep forest greens deepened to black. A moment of homesickness overtook me, and I sighed, poignantly longing for cultivated farmland stretching to a broad horizon with fields of patchwork green and yellow. What a contrast this crude mining town was to Hartford, with its white clapboard houses and elm-lined streets. It was already warm in Kansas, and by the Fourth of July corn tassels would dance in the bright clear sun and people would gather in the park to celebrate. How could Aunt

Esther have left all that for this raw and uncivilized place?

Everything in the harsh landscape made me feel intimidated and uneasy. Even the expressions on the people walking in and out of the buildings and scurrying along wooden sidewalks seemed to me to be as harsh and formidable as this frontier town in which they lived. The buggy rolled past the stone building on the corner of Main and King streets and I read a gold-leafed sign: "Halstead Bank." "You . . . own the bank?"

A peculiar expression crossed his face; a shadow darkened his features. "Not anymore. I had to sell my shares . . . because of some financial reversals."

"Oh, I'm sorry," I stammered, cursing my blunder.

"It's only temporary," he said without easing the sudden brooding in his tight lips. "A run of bad luck shut down the Goldstock—that's my mine—and I've had to liquidate some assets to meet obligations on a new smelter I'm building. Once it's in operation, it will handle ore from mines all over these mountains. It'll make Glen Eyrie the hub for this area. I'll recover my losses quickly unless—" He broke off abruptly. "Enough of that. I'm sure your main concern is your aunt's welfare."

"Didn't she tell you I was coming?"

"No, I'm afraid she has always kept her own counsel, and of late she has been too ill for much conversation. You will find her quite changed." There was no mistaking the warning in his tone.

His words brought tears and an anxious tightening in my stomach. Memories of the soft smile, gentle hands, and shining eyes of my dear aunt washed over me. I had always adored her from the time my chubby legs could totter around in her wake. I blinked rapidly and stilled an impulse to tell him about the happy, outgoing Esther I knew. His somber expression stopped me. I must learn to hold my tongue. This man had a way of delving deeply into things which were none of his concern, and I distrusted him completely.

It took me a moment to compose myself. "I guess I'm a little homesick," I admitted.

He nodded. "I'm from New York . . . but I never get homesick for it."

"You were born there?"

"No . . . in a small village near London. My parents came to America when I was three years old. My father was an investment banker, and about ten years ago my parents decided to return to England. My younger brother went with them and I came west to seek my fortune . . . like your aunt and uncle. I decided to grubstake several prospectors, and hit with one of them. Took a lot of money out of the Goldstock . . . put a lot of it back into the town . . . and then a disastrous rock fall closed up the mine. Then's when I decided to put my assets into building a smelter. Fortunately the east-west railroad has been joined and goods can be transported from coast to coast. The need for ores and minerals and natural resources is going to grow . . . and the West is a treasure house." His gaze flickered across the craggy peaks and his eyes narrowed. "One thing about these mountains, they ensure the survival of the fittest." He was no longer smiling.

Survival of the fittest. His words lay coldly on my heart and caused me to lapse back into my mood of anxiety and suspicion. I was glad when he reined the gray horse in front of the small train station.

A fancy brougham with red wheels was parked there and a liveried coachman was helping a large woman into the carriage. Her elaborately dressed brassy-yellow hair looked like a bird's nest and even sprouted feathers in an adornment of clips and combs. An hourglass figure was tightly encased in a green velvet dress with silk polka-dot sleeves and overskirt. The coachman shut the door, climbed to his high perch, and in a moment the brougham jolted away. I glimpsed the young brunette girl from the train through a window as they passed, but I could not see if the mystery lady was in the fancy carriage too. Kipp saw my eyes following it and said, "That's Millie McCarthy. She must have picked up a new boarder for her sporting house."

I didn't respond, but felt a hot flush creeping up my neck. "You obviously knew one was arriving today," I retorted.

"Yes, and I do apologize . . . for my welcome." He peered at me sheepishly. "Of course, you got even with me—with the brandy."

My lips curved—I couldn't help it—as I remembered the way my drink had bathed his astonished face. A giggle bubbled up and then expanded into a full laugh. His mouth spread and he laughed with me. There was only companionable mirth between us—all else forgotten—until a woman's full, resonant voice cut through our laughter.

"I thought that was you, Kipp."

"Oh, hello, Lucretia." Kipp jumped down and looped the reins through a hitching ring. Still chuckling, he said, "May I introduce Esther's niece, Miss Allison Lacey, who's come all the way from Hartford, Kansas . . . and, Allison, this is Lucretia Poole, the sharpest, wiliest, most unscrupulous businesswoman you'd ever hope to meet." There were respect and affection in his tone.

Even in the dusky twilight, I could see that she was a handsome woman, dressed rather severely but with impeccable taste in a brown foulard jacket and skirt, softened by a buff linen vest with broad rolling collar. Under a simple high-crown bonnet, her deep brown hair was parted in the middle and pulled back over her ears. Green eyes as clear and cold as any I had ever seen surveyed me with the frank appraisal of a horse trader. She was nearly as tall as Kipp, and I decided her rigid carriage added another inch to her height. "How do you do," I said politely, and received a slight nod in return.

"Lucretia's husband was the prospector who made the lucky strike for us," Kipp said quickly. "And after his death, she took over his investments . . . and now owns half of the town. How's the opera house coming, Lucretia . . . is it going to make its opening date?"

"There are some problems. I thought we'd talk them over at dinner—that is, if our dinner date is still on?" She gave me a curt look.

"Of course, of course," Kipp said smoothly, and then turned to me. "Lucretia and I always have Friday-evening dinner together at my house," he explained to me, "so we can discuss some mutual business ventures afterward."

"I'm sure I will retire early . . . after I've seen my aunt." Fatigue must have been in my voice, for he nodded and said briskly that he would get my trunk and be back in a moment.

"And I must be on my way, too," Lucretia said. "I came down to pick up . . . a package. I shall look forward to getting acquainted at dinner, Miss Lacey." She gave me a smile that lacked any warmth. There was veiled antipathy in her manner as she moved away. I don't know what she said to Kipp Halstead, but as he turned under a lamplight, I saw his expression change. He nodded, gave a quick glance in my direction, and spoke rapidly to her.

I felt that tightening of skin that comes when you know people are talking about you. What was she saying to him? Kipp Halstead didn't appear to be the kind to take orders from any-one . . . but his behavior toward the Widow Poole had been almost obsequious. I didn't like it. I didn't like it all.

In a moment he was back. He put my small trunk and portmanteau on a rack and then guided the trim, high-stepping horse back to the center of town, turning in the opposite direction from the hotel. Music and laughter bounced out swinging saloon doors as we passed. Gaudily dressed women and staggering drunks seemed to be everywhere. I knew now why Miss Purcell had been aghast at my plans to come to a gold-mining town alone. I was grateful for my escort's presence and I gave him a feeble smile of gratitude.

"Sorry to take you past the Row," he said, "but there isn't much choice of streets. I'm afraid the respectable and the not-so-respectable businesses are all mixed in together. That's Millie's Gambling and Sporting House over there. She's getting ready for a big night."

"A friend of yours, I presume." Gravel in my tone.

He laughed. "Millie's everybody's friend—as long as somebody else is doing the buying. She pulls in gold nuggets faster than any hardworking prospector can dig them out . . . and is always bringing in new boarders for her loyal clientele."

The glimpse I'd gotten of the brassy-haired woman had fit with my reading about the madams who ran numerous brothels in Kansas City. Even though my curiosity wanted to know more, I knew it was not a proper subject of conversation. "Where is the new opera house going to be?"

"Across the creek. It's really going to be just a fancy playhouse. Lucretia has a melodrama troop from Denver all lined up for an opening-night gala." He cocked his handsome head and looked at me. "Might take you—as a kind of welcoming gesture."

"How kind . . . but I'm afraid I must decline

the invitation." My reply was even, but a spurt of excitement tingled through me.

"We'll talk about it later," he said with his usual arrogance.

The buggy clattered across a narrow wooden bridge spanning a white-foamed stream of water which I learned later was named Timber Creek. Once on the other side, we began to climb a very steep road that zigzagged back upon itself to gain altitude. I caught my breath as the valley floor dropped away. Clenching the sides of the seat as we lurched around hairpin curves, I gasped, "Where . . . where are we going?"

"Up there." He pointed to a promontory that rose out of a band of conifer trees, and I could see the faint silhouette of a rooftop against the purple-gray sky. I kept my eyes fixed on the horse's bobbing head, not trusting myself to look anyplace else.

When a two-story frame house came into view, I thought we'd reached his house, but he shook his head and said, "That's Lucretia's home . . . mine's on top of the ridge." We took another sharp curve and I nearly fainted as the buggy almost lurched off the narrow road. I wondered if he was deliberately reining the horse so dangerously close to the edge. Was he trying to frighten me? I clamped my jaw shut, vowing we could plunge over the side of the cliff before I would utter one sound.

As if amused by my stoic manner, he said in a conversational tone, "Back in those trees, I built my first cabin . . . lived in it three years before the Goldstock mine changed my fortune. If things don't get better for me, I may have to move back into it."

I wanted to ask him some personal questions, for this was the second time he had referred to some financial crisis. Of course, I couldn't, but as soon as I found out what the situation was with my aunt, I was determined that neither of us would be a burden on him. I barely had enough money to get back home, but surely Aunt Esther had not lost everything. If she had sold the hotel, then there must be some money. My thoughts must have communicated themselves to him, for he said pleasantly, "You will like my home, a mixture of Queen Anne and Victorian. I brought most of the furnishings from New York."

I had just about despaired of ever reaching it when the horse mounted one last steep rise and the buggy rolled under a canopy of needled trees to a large house and adjoining outbuildings. Vaulting chimneys and a mansard roof rose jaggedly against a burnt-umber sky which was rapidly losing all color to an invading blackness.

As we approached the house, I saw that it had been built so that there was a wide expanse of ground in front of it. The back of the house, however, and one side had been built on the precipice, commanding a view of the valley floor and the wide gulch leading upward toward higher mountains. Amber light from a lamp inside the house gleamed through a downstairs window, but the watery light did not reach beyond the first gables. The second and third floors were lost in possessive shadows which made the structure appear darkly sinister. It emitted a cold welcome.

The long journey, a building anxiety over the condition of my aunt, and the jigsaw of emotions that had engulfed me since my arrival suddenly combined in an overpowering sense of apprehension—as if some sixth sense realized that the last moment had come when I could extricate myself from unseen webs of violence. I must have taken a tense breath, for he looked at me in surprise and glanced at the hand I had tightened in a fist on my lap.

"What is it? What's the matter?"

There were no words to describe the premonition. There was nothing to be afraid of . . . nothing tangible . . . only a subtle presentiment. But I was overtired, the long journey had brought forth a confusing array of emotions. My encounter with this magnetic stranger had tumbled my thoughts in confusion. It was natural that I was nervous coming to such a strange place. A feeling of panic was natural. And yet . . . I swallowed dryly.

"Are you fearful about Esther's condition?" he prodded.

I nodded because that was the easiest response—and in a way, a correct, if incomplete one.

"She's had good care. I've done as much for her as I could."

But had he? He now owned the hotel, which represented a lifetime of work and dreams.

At that moment a grinning Oriental man appeared silently out of the shadows and took the reins from Kipp's hands. "Ching Lee, this is Miss Lacey. She's going to be our guest. Take her things up to the front bedroom."

The small man nodded, bobbing his black queue.

Kipp alighted and came around the buggy to my side. "Ching's sister, SuLang, works in the house and has been looking after your aunt."

As he guided me to the ground, one hand rested lightly on mine and the other touched my waist with possessive firmness. His nearness sent my heart hammering under my rib cage. Why did I let him pulverize me like this? I had thought myself above such irrational behavior, but as he bent over me, his handsome face near mine, a peculiar exhilaration assaulted me. My only defense was to remember that somehow he had cheated my aunt out of the hotel. I must not let his charm put me off guard. I pulled back. "Before we go in, I would like to know what methods you used to make my aunt sell out to you."

"Are you always judge and jury . . . before the evidence is in?" he challenged.

"I trust my instincts," I countered.

"Good." His mobile mouth instantly spread in an infuriating grin. "I like the way your instincts react, Allie," he said in an intimate tone.

Allie! I was furious! No one had ever dared pin that horrid nickname on me. Words caught in my throat. I brushed past him up the flagged walk to mount the wide steps to the wide porch, my skirts rustling briskly across the smooth, flat stones. Subdued light filtered through leaded glass panes on each side of the door, and I could see the glow of a lamp inside. My former sense of foreboding faded as quickly as it had come. Now that I could see the white clapboards of the house and the decorative railings and columns, I knew that it was a lovely house. I felt foolish that I had reacted so negatively to it.

He opened the door to a spacious entry. It was of baronial proportions, but empty, and it echoed with our footsteps. Suddenly the promise of warmth receded. A closed-up mustiness bit my nostrils and I saw that all but one of the doors opening along a wide hall were closed. The lamp I'd seen through the beveled glass at the front door was the only one burning. A hall receded into blackness toward the back of the house. Dark walnut wainscoting on the walls was unpolished, and ornate moldings held a layer of dust. A dull wine carpet runner was laid upon stairs which vanished into the darkness above. The somber atmosphere was oppressive. The air held a stale, unpleasant odor, as if no windows or doors had been opened to freshen it. There was no hint of beeswax, no starched curtains. The truth was clear: this was not a home with a personality of its own and all its embracing smells. It did not emit any feeling of welcome or warmth. I shivered as if some terrible unhappiness permeated the air, and I felt threatened within its walls.

Suddenly I heard muffled sounds of someone

running from the back of the house. I took a step backward and stiffened, wondering what kind of creature was rushing at us from the gloomy back hall.

In the next instant a relieved gasp parted my lips. A small boy bounded into the front hall, stopping short when he saw us. Dark-haired, he had a small, tense face, and his expression was wary and guarded, as if he were prepared to turn on his heel and flee.

"Come here, Philippe. This is my son. Say hello to Miss Lacey."

His son! I couldn't understand my intense reaction. A blow to the stomach could not have been any more devastating. He was married! He had a wife! A deep sense of betrayal mocked me. Then sanity asserted itself. Of course, what more could I expect? I scolded myself. And why should it make the least bit of difference to me? From the first moment he had touched me, I had not trusted him. Why was I entertaining this sense of devastation? The boy was dressed in short brown pants, white shirt, and wrinkled black socks above high button shoes. His clothes were clean and fairly new, but there was still something of the urchin about him.

"Come here," his father repeated, "and meet Miss Lacey."

Forgetting my own bewilderment, I became aware of the boy's discomfort. I smiled and moved forward. "Hello, Philippe. I'm happy to meet you."

"You're not old," he said accusingly, "like the other Miss Lacey."

I smiled but his father said gruffly, "Say 'how do you do' and then run and tell Tooley we have a guest for dinner."

The boy mumbled, "How do you do, Miss Lacey." There was no affectionate welcome for his father as he glared at him and spat, "Tooley's drunk." He turned and fled.

Kipp sighed heavily. "Sometimes I find a seven-year-old beyond my understanding . . . especially one who lies and steals." A flicker of something like pain creased his forehead. He was no longer the suave, arrogant Kipp Halstead I had met at the hotel. He was a man . . . a father . . . who desperately needed to share a deep problem.

"At school we found that such behavior was often a sign of emotional turmoil," I offered weakly.

"Yes, I'm afraid you're right," he murmured.

"What does your wife think?" I inquired in a tone I hoped was professional. I often had to counsel with parents about an obstreperous child.

"I don't have a wife . . . and Philippe doesn't have a mother."

"I see." Was that a hint of relief I felt?

He spread his hands in a helpless gesture. "And that, my dear Miss Lacey, may state the problem quite succinctly, don't you agree?"

I lowered my eyes, confused by my feelings. I wanted to reach up and soothe that brow. "Perhaps with time . . ." I said vaguely.

He recovered himself. "Well, now, I'm sure you're anxious to see Esther."

"Yes, please."

"I will have your things put in the front guestroom . . . across the hall from mine," he said as we mounted the staircase. Was there a glint of amusement that deepened the gray of his eyes—a challenge, perhaps?

I chose to ignore it and stiffened, as much against the betrayal of my own feelings as at any forwardness on his part. I said briskly, "I must impose upon your hospitality until I can determine my aunt's condition . . . and make our plans accordingly." My tone was one I used arranging next term's schedule with an administrator.

"My home is your home."

I found the polite response facetious and I had to bite back an angry retort that it would seem that our hotel was also his hotel!

When we reached the top of the stairs, I was once more aware of the deserted feeling of the house. The atmosphere was as oppressive here as it had been on the main floor. Every door along the hallway was closed, and only a couple of sconces had been filled with oil and lit. Smudges of feeble light did little to alleviate the suffocating gloom of the hallway. There was no warmth here, only an invading coldness that made me shiver.

"Esther's room is at the back of the house," he said. "It is closer to the servants' stairs and easier for SuLang to see to her needs. As you've probably noticed, we live in only a few rooms in the house. If I had known you were coming—"

"I wouldn't want to cause any extra work or inconvenience for anyone," I responded, and tried not to let the insidious gloom and shadows affect me, but even before I entered my aunt's room, the house had done its work. My mouth was dry, my palms moist, and my spirits leadened.

The room was dimly lighted by a small brass-fitted lamp that stood on a pedestal table. A small wick flamed inside the lamp's green glass bowl, and muted light flickered upon the dark woodwork and embossed wallpaper. Near the four-poster bed, a quiet figure sat in a motionless rocking chair.

"Remember," Kipp said gently, "your aunt . . . is not herself. The blow on her head has left her . . . disoriented. Sometimes she's rational, and sometimes she's not."

I approached the gray-haired woman, my heart thumping loudly. The shock of her frail passiveness paralyzed me for a moment. The years had put their mark upon her. I had expected that, but it was her vacant, unseeing stare that brought my hand against my mouth in a smothered sob. Aunt Esther had always been so full of life that laughter bubbled easily from her lips. Even when things went wrong, optimism was her first reaction and she had often brushed away my childish tears with the promise that all would be well, given time. I tried to cling to this homily as I approached her, tears in my eyes.

Was this the sunny, fair-haired, laughing aunt who had enveloped me in loving arms and made me feel that the world was bright and lovely? Memories flooded back: summer picnics, hand-made Christmas gifts of soft wool and embroidered lace, a new puppy hidden in the barn and then thrust laughingly into my arms. The empty place in my life had never been filled after my aunt and uncle had left. I had grown into womanhood, and eventually time, distance, and responsibilities had come between us, but the aching emptiness had always continued. Then her frantic letters had drawn us back together, and I knew that whatever evil had engulfed my aunt, I was here to share it.

I took one of the clammy hands. "I came, Aunt Esther . . . I came."

Wide eyes like those of an unblinking china doll turned slowly upon my face. Her glazed stare showed no sign of recognition.

"It's me . . . Allison." I leaned forward and kissed her cheek. "I'm here . . ." I let myself sink down on the floor and put my head on her lap. My eyes filled and overflowed unabashedly down my cheeks. I did not know when Kipp quietly left.

4

*T*HE sound of an ormolu clock's quiet ticking mingled with my quiet sobs until I began to collect myself and the shock of Aunt Esther's condition began to ebb. I should have expected it, I reasoned. Her frantic, sprawling notes were evidence enough that she was not herself, but I had foolishly expected to find Aunt Esther the way she had been when she kissed me good-bye: strong, determined, with a proud lift to her golden head radiating confidence. This quiet, pathetic shell of a woman with a tracery of purple veins in her pale, translucent skin tore at my heart. A physical illness would have been easier to bear; at least I could have nursed her back to health. Then I reminded myself that Kipp had said she had moments of lucidity. Perhaps with me here, they would increase and she would become her old self again. As if to verify my thoughts, one of her hands moved to touch my head, which still lay in her lap. My heart leapt as she began to stroke my hair.

I looked up and searched her face hopefully.

Blue eyes the color of wild windflowers held a glint of puzzlement instead of the glazed unseeing look. "It's me, Allison," I said with a rush, excited by the change in her expression.

Her lips curved slightly as she said in a clear voice I remembered so well, "You'd better hurry, child . . . you're going to be late for school."

I bit my lip, fighting back the sudden fullness in my eyes. I clasped her hand and said as evenly as my emotion would allow, "I'm a teacher now, Aunt Esther . . . remember, you wrote to me at Miss Purcell's . . . asked me to come here to Glen Eyrie . . ."

Her forehead furrowed as if she were trying to drag some memory up out of a confused, murky pool. "Allison?"

"Yes, I'm here now, Aunt Esther . . . in Glen Eyrie."

Her chest suddenly rose and fell with the rapid breathing of a frightened bird. "No!" she cried. "I was wrong! You shouldn't have come!"

"It's all right, Aunt Esther." I tried to pat her hand, but she jerked it away from me.

Her eyes jerked wildly as if warding off some approaching danger. "You must go!" Her cries became a high-pitched shriek. "Go . . . go!"

I tried to put my arms around her shoulders, but she lurched to her feet, wavering, frantically pushing at me.

"Allison, go . . . before it's too late!" Her voice rose in a frenzied pitch; her clawlike hands pushed me back. I did not know whether to stay in the room and try to calm her rising agitation or leave. The decision was taken out

51

of my hands as a youthful Asian girl rushed into the room.

Dressed in a simple Oriental dress with high neck and straight lines, she moved quickly and silently on soft black shoes and gathered my aunt into her arms. Her slanted dark eyes, rounded cheeks, and bowed mouth were the pleasing features of a girl in her early teens. Instantly Aunt Esther's high-pitched cries changed into a whimpering as the girl spoke to her. I could not understand what she was saying to my aunt, but her tone was gentle and soothing and Aunt Esther let herself be guided back to her chair.

I let out my breath and was about to murmur a word of gratitude when the girl raised her eyes and looked directly into mine. I had never seen such raw malevolence before in my life. Her black eyes were points of honed steel. "Missy, go," she said in a tone as deadly as a snake's rattle.

I automatically took a step backward and then stammered, "I . . . I didn't mean to upset her."

"You go way . . . I take care . . . good care."

My words tumbled over themselves as I explained I had come at my aunt's bidding. "I want to help. . . . Please, tell me what I can do."

"Missy come too late! I mail letters, but you no come. All the time my lady waits for you . . . now too late."

Sobs crowded up in my throat, but I swallowed them back. "I wanted to come . . . but I couldn't," I explained to the girl as if I were addressing a jury. "I had no money until I completed my teaching contract. Do you understand? I wrote that I would come as soon I could—"

"Missy come too late." It was a judgment that invited no defense.

My aunt was quiet now, sitting back in her chair. The girl's reassuring hand was on her shoulder. I was shut out. My presence was an unwanted intrusion. The girl's unblinking gaze stabbed at me. There was nothing I could do but turn and leave.

With tears burning my eyes, I walked blindly down the cold, dim hall until I came to an open door. My trunk and portmanteau had been set in the front bedroom. It smelled like it hadn't been aired in weeks, and I assumed it had been shut off like most of the rooms in the rest of the house. A lamp with etched-glass shades had been lit, but no fire had been laid in the elegant small fireplace.

I hugged myself in the penetrating coldness. A few pieces of kindling lay on the hearth and I sniffed back my tears and laid a fire, finding a small box of wooden matches on the mantel. A moment later, greedy, curling tongues licked the wood. My spirits always found solace from a leaping fire. Some primeval remembrance, perhaps. As I felt its warmth, my fragmented emotions began to heal.

I looked about the room. There had been no time to turn it out properly. I felt like an intruder who had come uninvited and without proper announcement. A wash of homesickness swept over me. What was I doing in this house, alone and unwanted? I did not belong here. Dust upon the furniture mocked my presence.

A huge bed with thick carved legs dominated the room—my small cot at the school could have fit three times across it! Lamplight showed wallpaper sprigged in blue and yellow. Lancet windows with small panes were dressed with lace curtains, and full blue plush drapes had been loosened from twisted gold cords and drawn across the windows. I wondered if SuLang had been preparing the room when my aunt's shrieks brought her down the hall. The furniture, fashioned with delicate carvings and inlaid with mahogany and birch, was in need of a good polishing with beeswax and turpentine, I noted as I ran my finger over a dusty tabletop. If this was the guestroom, it was obvious that visitors to the house were not frequent. A sense of isolation was exaggerated by my weariness.

I sat down on the edge of the bed and stared at a floral Aubusson rug that must have cost a fortune. I wondered if empty rooms lay behind most of the closed doors or if they were furnished as elaborately as this one. It was possible that financial reversals might have caused Kipp to sell off most of the furnishings. It appalled me to think that all these things had been laboriously hauled to this high crest in the Rocky Mountains. Most of it must have come by mule train. Remembering the steep, rugged slopes and mountain passes, I marveled that any of it had arrived intact.

I wanted nothing more than to lie back on the soft feather mattress and close my eyes, but the memory of my aunt's pitiful cries and the Oriental girl's animosity chided me out of my tiredness. I pulled out Aunt Esther's last letter from my recticule. "I fear for my life . . . please come . . . you are my only hope." It was dated three months earlier, before her injury. Had she fallen . . . or been assaulted? In those few moments of lucidity when my aunt recognized me, I knew she feared for my safety. Her agitated cries of "Go . . . go . . ." were born of some terror, and she wished to protect me from the evil that had overcome her. But I would not go, and now that I was here, I must begin to take hold. If I were patient, I could reach her, and when she realized I was here, she might lose her fears.

I wanted to talk to Kipp. Even though my presence at the dinner table tonight would be an intrusion, I would not cower in my room. I must speak to him about Aunt Esther and judge for myself what really had happened.

The decision made, new energy dissipated my weariness. I unpacked a few of my clothes and some personal items, which I placed in a spacious wardrobe and on a lady's dressing table that had a matching Hepplewhite stool. My host had not said anything about dressing for dinner, but the genteel furnishings of my bedroom indicated that perhaps social graces as well as beautiful Victorian and Queen Anne furniture had been transported from New York to this mountain town. I even discovered a bathroom a few steps down the hall, with a marble sink and a deep zinc bathtub.

After refreshing myself with delightfully warm water, I changed into my second-best gown, which I had fashioned from a pattern offered in a recent issue of the *Delineator*. Miss Purcell said its deep forest-green color was flattering to my clear ivory skin and the reddish highlights in my amber hair. I liked the tapering bodice and flared peplum, which nicely shaped my bust and waist. The mock bustle draping, trimmed with rouleau satin ribbon, was rather saucy, I thought. I usually wore this dress on visiting days, when it was necessary to mingle with parents and serve tea to the school patrons. I told myself that I wasn't dressing for Kipp Halstead, but my fingers fumbled nervously with the clasps. I wondered what Lucretia Poole would be wearing. What was the real relationship between her and Kipp? Was it purely business? I remembered the way her clear eyes had assessed my face and figure. Even though there had been no hint of coquetry in her manner, a subtle hint of possessiveness had been there.

As I brushed my hair back into its usual smooth twist, I remembered how Kipp's lips had felt against mine and the way an indescribable warmth had fled into my limbs. In the mirror a blush crept up into my face as I relived his embraces. My whole body remembered the tantalizing pressure of his chest and thighs pressed against mine. This arousal was new to me . . . and frightening!

A foolish hammering under my rib cage

betrayed my nervousness as I descended the stairs into the murky hall with its one low-burning lamp. My high, soft shoes echoed on the floor as I walked across the foyer to the only open door letting light into the hall. As I stepped inside, the now familiar spicy, outdoor scent of the master of the house permeated the air, but he was not in sight. Soft lamplight pervaded the room, and masculine colors and leather furniture lent a comfortable, lived-in look unlike the dismal air of the rest of the house. Almost furtively I glanced about at bookshelves filled with expensive leather-bound volumes. Many of the volumes were my favorites—especially those containing the poetry of John Donne and the Brownings. My own cheap copies were well-worn and I longed to hold these gold-leafed volumes in my hands and finger the crisp vellum pages. I was surprised to see Mark Twain's just-released *Innocents Abroad* lying on a library table with a bookmark in it.

I hesitated to investigate farther, even though my curiosity was piqued. And then I caught my breath. I was suddenly aware that someone was in the room! A quick, traveling gaze about could not discern anyone. I took a few steps forward and waited. A soft shuffle behind a large oak desk jerked my eyes in that direction. I moved forward and peered around it. Kipp's seven-year-old son was cowering there, sitting on the floor. A glass case behind him containing rock and mineral specimens was open, and several of the ore samples were scattered in his lap and on the floor beside him. His wide, unsmiling eyes fixed on me like an animal about to spring.

"Hello, there. What are you doing, Philippe?" My tone was meant to sound friendly, but it brought a leap of fear to his eyes and an aggressive twist to his lips.

"My father said I could play with them!"

My teaching experience identified the nervous twitch of a lie. "They're very pretty," I said, my voice void of any censure. "Rocks are interesting, don't you think? I don't know much about minerals, but I always thought it might be fun to collect them." I eased down on the edge of a nearby oval-back chair and pointed to one of the rocks in his hands. "I don't know what kind that is . . . do you?"

He looked ready to fling it at me but he mumbled, "Blue quartz."

"Really? I've never seen that color before. I thought quartz was white . . . like that one." I pointed to a cluster of clear crystals. "May I see it?"

I waited as some kind of mental battle waged within him and knew victory when he handed it to me. Turning it over in my hands, I watched him out of the corner of my eye. The boy remained stiff and alert, like a wild creature poised for flight. I handed back the blue quartz and pointed to a piece of sparkling ore in his lap. "Is that gold?"

My question seemed to relax his slim shoulders. There was a superior edge to his tone. "Can't you tell real gold from fool's gold?"

"It looks real to me . . . but I guess you don't have any gold nuggets to show me."

"No gold, but . . ." His thin hand reached into his pocket and he brought out a piece of amethyst. I felt a rush of joy when he readily held it out to me.

"It's beautiful," I murmured.

"That's amethyst . . . worth money too." His deep-set eyes flared at me under a fringe of long eyelashes, as if daring me to contradict him. His hands showed white knuckles as he gripped the lavender stone, and his glare was like that of a hostile animal. I didn't dare move an inch closer to him, even though I wanted to ruffle his hair and make him smile.

"That is a treasure," I agreed solemnly, and handed back the piece of amethyst. I watched him put it back in his pocket, his pugnacious stare daring me to object.

I smiled reassuringly, as if he had every right to take what he wanted from his father's collection.

I saw the corners of his mouth relax, as if a silent pact had been made between us. With an eagerness that belied his somber, pinched face, he told me about a place where you could find lots of specimens just by looking on the ground.

"Really?" I was honestly intrigued by the idea.

"I could show you where . . . if you wanted to hunt for some."

"All right, but I'll have to get permission from your father."

"He'll say no! He always says no. The only time I get to go anywhere is with Tooley."

"If it's safe, he'll let you go with me," I said with more confidence than I felt. "He knows I'm a teacher—"

"A teacher!"

I had to laugh at his grimace. I wondered what his brief experience with teachers had been. "Now, why don't you put everything back while I find your father and see if it's time for dinner." I stood up, gave him another smile, and turned away, making a mental note to come back later to see if the amethyst specimen was back in the case, remembering his father had said he stole and lied.

As I returned to the hall, closed doors on both sides intrigued me. Were they all empty of furniture? Was the house only a shell? Curiosity made me turn the doorknob on the closest one. In the dim wash of lamplight from the hall, I could see that the room was a large parlor. Moonlight poured through high windows and touched everything with an eerie patina. The large room was far from empty: classical chairs, brocaded sofas, and parlor tables with lamps were arranged in groups on the floor. Overhead a huge chandelier tinkled slightly from an unseen movement of cold air and caught light from the hall in its dusty prisms. It should have been a room filled with laughter, conversations, and sparkling goblets. Instead the room whispered of neglect and an overpowering sadness. Moving shadows coming through the windows played along the floor like a waiting beast, hushed but alive in the silence of the room.

I could not identify the presentiment that

tugged at me. I had never thought myself en-
dowed with any psychic powers, but at that
moment I braced myself against a sense of chilling evil that suddenly threatened to engulf me.
Shaken and bewildered, I slammed the door
shut and stilled an urge to bolt up the stairs to
the warmth of my room.

Then my ears picked up voices floating down
the hall. It sounded as if someone had just
come into the house—perhaps a side entrance,
I thought, as I heard Lucretia's clear, crisp greeting and Kipp's response. The sound of their
normal voices mocked my melodramatic behavior. Fatigue must have loosened my imagination. The premonition I had experienced in the
deserted room now slid away and I gave a short
laugh. I smoothed my skirts and touched my
hair nervously. Then I moved forward toward
the voices.

They led me to a room in the depths of the
house. I paused in the doorway to get my bear-
ings. I viewed a small sitting room, and beyond
it, through open double doors, a small morning
room with a modest round oak table and wooden
chairs. We obviously were not going to dine in
any elegant dining room. With this knowledge
came the embarrassment that I was completely
overdressed! I saw that Lucretia had only removed her long-waisted jacket and hat. Her
deep brown hair was caught in a smooth chi-
gnon just above a collar of lace ruching that
graced her long neck. Kipp had replaced his
sportsman's jacket with a plain fawn-colored

coat which molded his shoulders in the same provocative fashion. They stood with their backs to me and were not aware of my presence for a moment as I hung back and wondered if I should dash back upstairs and change into one of my serge skirts and shirtwaists.

"I don't know why you put up with it," Lucretia said. "It's a disgrace, that man drunk again!"

"So it seems. I guess it was about time for Tooley to lay on a good one," answered Kipp in a matter-of-fact tone which was in sharp contrast to Lucretia's.

"What about dinner?" Her tone was edged with impatience.

Kipp shrugged. "I poured some hot coffee down him about an hour ago . . . he may rise to the occasion yet," he said with an amused laugh. "And don't sell that Irishman short, he's a better chef dead drunk than most cooks are stone sober."

"Well, my cook is reliable. If it weren't for your unexpected guest, we could go to my place . . ."

The disparaging emphasis on "guest" brought me forward without further thought. "Good evening," I said politely.

Kipp's eyes traveled over me and brought heat up in my face as he grinned appreciatively.

"Is there some problem?" I asked pointedly. I was certainly capable of fixing my own meal, and these two could go and do . . . whatever they did at their Friday-night dinners.

"A slight delay, perhaps," he said smoothly. "May I offer you a sherry?"

"No, thank you." I said it quite primly and properly but the knowing twinkle in his eye brought back the laughter we'd shared about my tossed drink. For a moment our eyes met and all the lectures I had given myself about this man were lost. What was the matter with me? He smiled and my self-discipline dissolved. It was all I could do to look away from him and sit down in the closest chair.

"Since you dressed so elaborately for dinner," Lucretia said, her smile condescending, "I assume Kipp didn't tell you that we don't stand on ceremony here." She took the drink that Kipp handed her. It looked and smelled suspiciously like straight whiskey. Once more I was aware of her large green eyes and high molded cheeks in a face which the sun had lightly tanned. "Social amenities have little place here in Glen Eyrie."

"Really? I didn't know polite amenities were ever out of place," I said sweetly. I thought I heard Kipp chuckle.

"I understand you're a schoolmarm."

Her tone was deprecating and I felt my ire rising. I was proud of my position at the school. I liked being a teacher, and I thought I was a good one. I had made my own way, taken control of my own life. My independence was something I treasured. I wasn't going to let this woman make me feel apologetic.

"Yes, I teach literature and composition at an academy for young women."

"Oh, one of those horrid finishing schools."

"I find nothing horrid about a liberal-arts education."

"Liberal arts," she scoffed. "Needlepoint and nice little tunes on a harpsichord is more like it."

"We do include music . . . and some other things like good manners," I said pointedly, and once more I thought I heard a chuckle issuing from Kipp's deep chest.

"I gained my education in the real world . . . the kind that really matters," snapped Lucretia.

"A self-made woman, that's Lucretia Poole," said Kipp, toasting her with his drink. I thought there was a subtle edge of irony to his tone, but his expression was unreadable. "Tell Allison how you managed your father's chandlery store from the time you were twelve years old."

"It's true," she said with a proud lift of her head. "My father retired young as a successful sea captain and went into business in Newport. The first words and numbers I learned were on ship invoices. I had two brothers who should have learned the business . . . but no, they had to be seamen . . . they went off and got themselves drowned." Her tone was more of censure than regret. "After my mother's death, I took over the house as well as the management of the store."

I was curious to know what events had brought her here. The Colorado Rockies were a far distance from the Atlantic seacoast. Before I could pose a question to satisfy my curiosity, the sound of a dinner bell came from the recesses of the kitchen.

"Well, I'll be damned," Kipp swore. "That boiled black coffee I poured down Tooley must have had its effect." He laughed, and the affection in his voice was obvious. "Shall we go, ladies, and see what our blurry-eyed cook has prepared?"

Kipp gallantly guided us into the morning room and pulled out a chair for each of us at the round table set with heavy white crockery on a floral tablecloth. He took a place halfway between us and made a facetious remark about a thorn between two roses.

"Isn't Philippe going to eat with us?" I asked, feeling that my presence put the table out of balance.

"He prefers to eat in the kitchen with Tooley when I have guests," he said smoothly, but I thought his eyes shuttered with the same pain I had seen earlier. "And SuLang always takes Esther a tray. Dr. Yates will look in on her tomorrow, and I'm sure you have some questions to ask him."

"Yes. I was curious about SuLang . . ."

"Didn't your aunt ever mention her or Ching Lee? I'm surprised. They were orphaned when their father was killed working on the narrow-gauge railroad coming up from Denver City. Esther and Benjamin took them in. I guess they must have been about eight and ten years old. They were grateful for a home, and both worked hard at the hotel . . . and when it was closed, I brought them here."

"That's Kipp," scoffed Lucretia. "He's not got enough troubles of his own . . . he had to borrow them."

"Now, Lucretia, don't give us one of your lectures. Esther and Allison are welcome guests in my house, and Ching Lee and SuLang earn their keep."

She scoffed. "How is your aunt this evening?"

"I . . . I'm afraid my presence upset her," I said, and a flush of emotions choked into my chest. I had wanted to talk to Kipp alone about her reaction, not in the presence of this austere woman who would undoubtedly consider any show of emotion as weakness.

"Then she knew you!" Kipp said, his face lighting up. "When I left the room, I was afraid that . . . that she wasn't going to respond. What did she say?"

"She called me by name . . . and then told me I was going to be late for school." My voice caught on an emotional snag, but I went on. "Then she seemed to understand that I was here now . . . in Glen Eyrie . . . and she became almost hysterical, screaming at me to go."

"Maybe you should," said Lucretia pointedly.

"I have no intention of leaving with my aunt in her present condition," I replied firmly. "She is the only family I have."

"No parents . . . brothers or sisters?"

"My parents have passed on, and I was an only child. And you, Mrs. Poole? Do you have a family?"

She didn't have time to respond, for at that moment the door to the kitchen swung open.

Naturally my curiosity had been piqued by all the references to the drunken Tooley. I expected to see some dissipated, blurry-eyed, sloppy drunk. Much to my surprise, a short, round-faced man looking a little like an overgrown leprechaun in western clothes bounced into the room. Dark suspenders ran over his checked shirt and held his pants up over his indefinable waistline. A pair of merry blue eyes set widely under busy eyebrows twinkled at me as he swung a huge tray around in a dramatic flourish and placed several steaming dishes on the table.

"A thousand pardons," he said in heavy Irish brogue. "Sure and I must be apologizing for the tardy dinner bell."

"How are you feeling, Tooley?" The question was sincere and it was obvious that Kipp cared for this funny little man a great deal.

"Some wee ones have taken up residence in me head and are playing the Angelus with hammers," he confessed wryly.

Kipp threw back his head and laughed. "I've never heard such a delightful description of a hangover. Now, let me present our houseguest, Allison Lacey . . . and this Irish renegade is Charlie O'Toole, known in these parts as Tooley. Best chef west of the Mississippi—when he's cooking and not swilling down Millie's best rotgut."

"Don't be shaming me in front of these lovely ladies. 'Twas cold medicine I was taking, to ward off a sickness in me lungs." But he winked at me as if sharing some private joke. "A bonny colleen ye are, with the gold and red of the sun in yer hair.''

"Watch him, Allie," warned Kipp, chuckling. "This lost son of Erin will charm you off your feet with his blarney."

I laughed, ignoring the fact that he presumptuously used my nickname. The obvious affection between the two men had somehow put life back on a sane and reassuring course. Even Lucretia's dominating and abrasive manner could not completely destroy it the rest of the meal. Tooley darted in and out of the kitchen, bringing chicken simmering in a white sauce with green leeks and bits of carrots. Homemade bread, thickly sliced, was offered with curls of butter and thick wild berry jam. The greens in the salad were mysterious but delicious, with egg-and-buttermilk dressing.

Kipp tried to keep the conversation general. He talked about the new president, General Grant, and his campaign promise to visit the West. "I hear one of the camps is going to lay a sidewalk of silver for him to walk on."

"Humph!" responded Lucretia. "We'd be better off to keep all the politicians as far east as possible. Let us govern ourselves the way we want. It's our right, after all. We're the ones who civilized the place."

They spoke of a miners' association which had been organized early in Glen Eyrie's history to decide on the size and number of claims each person could have and arbitrate water and gulch rights. Now the local government was a little more sophisticated, but the same people still ran the town. It was obvious that Kipp and Lucretia were included in that small number.

Lucretia asked Kipp pointed questions about his personal affairs. I learned that there had been all kinds of delays in completing the smelter. At times Kipp seemed lost in dark speculation. What dark worries did he hide behind that languid, debonair manner? Very deftly he turned the conversation away from his business concerns, and finally Lucretia seemed to realize he didn't want to talk about his affairs. I almost heard her sigh in resignation. She gave me a look which made it clear my presence at the table was an intrusion, one which they were forced to endure.

"Tell me, Mrs. Poole, how did you make your way to Glen Eyrie from New England?" I asked. Kipp had said when he introduced her that he had been business partners with her and her husband. I was more than curious about what had happened to Mr. Poole. "I imagine you miss the ocean—"

"Not at all!" She cut me off with a slice of her hand. "If I had wanted to stay in Newport, I could have. My father's chandlery store was prospering. I didn't have to sell out after Father died, but I persuaded my husband, Tim, that our future lay elsewhere. Tim lacked any sense of adventure, I'm afraid. He would have been content to be a seaman all his life," she scoffed, "but I knew that wealth didn't lie in whaling schooners or in selling hemp and brined fish. Tim didn't want to come, but once we got here, he found out that I had made the right decision."

But he's dead, I thought. How can she congratulate herself for making the move? There must have been something in my expression that made Kipp a little uncomfortable about the conversation. "It's too bad Tim couldn't have enjoyed the results of all his hard work," he offered. "If only he hadn't gone to Denver City in that blizzard."

She shrugged. "How was I to know that the train was going to get stuck . . . and he'd try to hike the rest of the way? If he'd stayed with the others in the train . . . But no, he had to be gallant!" Her tone was bitter. "Then he developed influenza and never did pick up the option on the land. I should have gone myself . . . then I wouldn't have lost both him and the land."

I couldn't tell from her tone which she hated losing more.

Kipp sought my eyes. "It was a real tragedy— Tim was one of the nicest men I ever met."

"This is no place for people who can't take care of themselves," Lucretia said crisply. "I'm afraid your aunt and uncle have found that out. Only the strongest will survive here."

"My aunt and uncle never turned away from hardships of any kind," I countered. "Before they moved to Hartford, they managed a three-hundred-acre farm. Then they moved to town, and Uncle Benjamin worked at a mill and Aunt Esther took in boarders—and raised me. Whatever bad luck befell them here was not their fault!"

She shrugged. "I think their grandiose ideas

invited trouble. All that nonsense about fancy cuisine, wine cellars, and elaborate Victorian furnishings. It was all that remodeling that caused your uncle's death, you know."

"I don't think this is the time to discuss that, Lucretia," Kipp said, a flash of anger narrowing his lips.

But I wanted to know. "What happened? I never heard the particulars. Aunt Esther just wrote that there had been an accident."

"More like a heart attack, I'd say." Lucretia sniffed. "He was carrying a bunch of stuff from the cellar out to the ravine to dump, and must have gotten dizzy and fallen. He tumbled about fifty feet . . . broke his neck."

Kipp's hand suddenly covered mine. "I'm sorry, Allison. I thought you knew."

I bit my lip and fought to maintain my composure. Lucretia didn't notice my reaction and continued to talk. "When bad luck settles on a place, it's better to get rid of it!" She seethed. "Why Kipp wanted to take it on, I'll never know. And now he's turning his house into a kind of retreat. Poor darling, he's had nothing but bad luck since he brought your aunt here. Bad luck sometimes follows certain people."

"Don't be ridiculous, Lucretia!"

"The facts speak for themselves, and the sooner Miss Lacey and her aunt return to Kansas, the better it will be for everyone." Her ice-cold green eyes held a message which I could not quite interpret. But there was no mistake about the venom in her look.

In less than two hours three people had told

me to leave. Maybe four, I thought as I caught Kipp's deep eyes, suddenly pensive and cold. As if to verify my thoughts, he said without a hint of his usual grin, "Lucretia may be right. You're welcome to my hospitality as long as you wish to stay. But there's very little you can accomplish."

"That's where you're wrong. I may be able to accomplish a great deal . . . more than anyone might like," I bragged foolishly. Suddenly I felt strong in my own youth, strong in my own intelligence, and strong in the love I held for my aunt. Even in my fear there was strength. "I intend to find out the truth about what has happened here—and who's responsible!"

Their silence was as cold and damp as the rest of the house.

5

I excused myself and fled upstairs. When I checked on Aunt Esther, I found her already in bed and asleep. Her gray hair was plaited neatly along each cheek. Her tranquil expression soothed my nerves and I kissed her cheek affectionately. SuLang was not in sight; I wondered which room in the dark corridor was hers. Tomorrow I would talk with the doctor. If he said Aunt Esther was well enough to travel, I would try to find the means to take her home. Miss Purcell had promised to mail my summer check in a few weeks—but even a few days seemed too long to wait, in view of the explosive reaction I had to Kipp Halstead. One touch and all rational thought sped from my head.

I knew that it was folly to stay here under his roof, but what choice did I have? Asking Kipp for a loan seemed highly presumptuous when all indications were that he was in financial straits. But he might be so relieved to have us out of his house that he would be willing to advance me the price of our train tickets and some travel money. Perhaps Aunt Esther had some money from the sale of the hotel that Kipp was handling for her. Why did this thought sent a soft-footed shiver up my spine? Surely I didn't think he had manipulated her into signing the hotel over to him for a negligible sum? Yes, I did think that, although unwillingly, but it seemed a possibility that could not be ignored. Yes, I must ask him about my aunt's financial condition—but would I know if he were lying to me? I doubted it. Where Mr. Kipp Halstead was concerned, I seemed to have tossed all rational thought to the wind.

I returned to my room and found that the bed had been turned down and warming bricks placed under the mound of covers. SuLang? I wished I had asked more about her, but there had been little opportunity, with Lucretia dominating the table conversation. I wondered how long the two of them would stay downstairs talking . . . and if Kipp usually saw her home . . . and if he might spend the night at her house. I could not tell exactly what their relationship entailed. At times Lucretia almost preened when he gave her his attention, as if confident that he was a moth to her flame. She tried to dominate him, and he listened to what she had to say but gave every indication that he made his own decisions. And yet he was deferential, respectful, and in some ways affectionate. I couldn't help but wonder if the woman didn't have some hold on him.

Today's scenes rose and fell in a kaleidoscope of emotions as I changed into my soft flannel gown and crawled into the wide, high bed. It seemed years ago instead of just this morning that I had changed trains at Denver City. Could maturity come upon a person in one day? It seemed to me that it could. After my parents had died and the farm sold for little more than the mortgage, the school had become my home. I had become secure in the well-ordered daily routines of a schoolmistress, even though I found the days tedious and secretly rebelled against my youth passing in such a dull fashion. I had thought myself quite grown-up, a proper chaperon for giggling, insipid young girls—and now I found that I might be the most vulnerable of all of them. Before today, I had never touched the wells of my feelings. I had taught romantic literature to my starry-eyed pupils and never once realized what a man's kisses could do to my latent desires.

Even my romance this past winter with another teacher, Emmett Hadley, who had joined the staff as the music instructor, had not prepared me for the exploding responses I felt in Kipp's arms. Emmett had given me a few furtive kisses in the shadows of my building the last time he took me home from a musicale, but his embrace had seemed more clumsy and embarrassing than anything. I had promised to write to him—but I knew that today's events could never be committed to pen and paper.

I closed my eyes. Tomorrow would be soon enough to sort everything out. I could not hold fatigue at bay any longer and gave myself up to blessed sleep.

Sometime past midnight I was awakened by a high-pitched cry reverberating throughout the house. Aunt Esther!

I leapt from the bed, grabbed my wrapper, and ran from the room. No, it wasn't my aunt! The cry was coming up the stairway from the main floor. At that instant Kipp brushed past me, his brocade dressing robe flapping like maroon wings as he took the stairs with a rush.

"What is it?" I gasped, dashing down after him at a reckless speed.

"Philippe . . ."

With me dogging his heels, he ran down the hall to the back of the house, past the morning room and kitchen, and to a wing that obviously was built for servants' quarters. The cries had lessened to whimpers and I could hear Tooley's strong Irish brogue in a soft murmuring. We reached the room where the Irishman was sitting on the edge of a narrow bed with his arms around the boy, rocking him gently.

"Nightmare," he mouthed to Kipp as we stood in the doorway. Kipp nodded and we stayed where we were—outside the room.

As Tooley lowered the sleeping boy back on the pillow, I whispered to Kipp, "What's he doing down here, and not in his own bed?"

Kipp closed his eyes for a moment and then said wearily, "It was his choice. He wouldn't stay in his room next to mine. Every night he'd sneak down here to be near Tooley. Finally I gave up. If this is where he'd rather be . . ." His voice trailed away.

" 'Twas another bad dream, poor wee lad,"

Tooley whispered as he came out of the room. He shook his head and padded back to his room across the hall. In his long underwear he was a comical figure and I smiled silently, entertaining a combination of embarrassment and amusement at the sight.

Quietly Kipp went in and stared down at his son. Philippe's dark eyelashes fringed his pale cheeks. With those dark, guarded eyes closed, he looked like a child to be hugged, squeezed, and nuzzled with kisses until he squealed with delight. His thin arms lay on top of the covers; his small hands were relaxed. Kipp bent over and kissed his forehead. I wondered how many kisses he stole in this furtive fashion.

Feeling like an intruder, I turned away, my eyes suspiciously moist, and had just reached the newel post at the bottom of the stairs when Kipp caught up with me. The dim glow of the hall lamp sent our shadows wavering in weird shapes upon the wall.

He apologized as he ran an agitated hand through thatches of tousled dark hair. "I'm sorry you were disturbed, Allison."

"It's all right. I thought it was Aunt Esther. Does Philippe have nightmares like that often?"

"Yes," he sighed wearily. "If you want to hear a long story . . ."

How could I turn away from his need to talk to someone? That absurd impulse to smooth his furrowed brow overtook me again. I nodded and we moved toward the library. Once more the insidious cold and gloom of the house enveloped me. I felt an invisible net settling over me—as if it were already too late to turn and flee.

In the library he struck a light to a hanging lamp and quickly added wood to the red embers of the fire. The room held a warmth which indicated he had been here earlier. I saw then that the Mark Twain book had been moved from the table and lay on the seat of a chair near the fire. The sight sent a spurt of foolish joy through me. He had not gone home with Lucretia!

I sat down on the leather couch as he knelt by the fire and used a bellows to fan it into a bright flame. His face caught a burnished light and for a moment the same vulnerability I had seen on Philippe's face flickered there. When he turned and smiled at me, a peculiar fluttering took me by surprise.

I knew it improper to remain in a man's company in my night attire. Although my wrapper was buttoned high with no sign of my flannel nightdress showing, the absence of undergarments was scandalous. Miss Purcell would have been horrified . . . but that dear lady seemed to be part of another world. I didn't care about social mores at the moment, I wanted to be here, with this man, sharing a burden that he seemed willing to share with me. As if reading my thoughts, he said with a wry smile, "This might appear to be a compromising situation, and if you'd rather not . . ."

"No, it doesn't matter." And I found to my surprise that it didn't.

He sat down in a nearby chair. "Good! That's

one thing I hated about New York society—ridiculous, hypocritical mores. Scandals were served up like delectable morsels at tittering tea parties.''

I couldn't help but wonder how often handsome Kipp Halstead figured in those scandals.

"Anyway, I came west to get away from all that," he continued. "When my father's health failed and he decided to take the family back to England, I headed for the frontier." He sighed. "My brother, Richard, should have been the elder son. He's the one willing to spend his life in stuffy offices, reading financial reports. My father and I have been at odds ever since I was old enough to play truant." He gave a short laugh. "I used to sneak out of the schoolroom and head for the docks. For hours I watched schooners set sail—used to think of running away to become a cabin boy on one of them. I'd probably have made a terrible sailor, though. I love the mountains more than the water. Anyway, I came to Colorado to seek my fortune. I made money, too, but it wasn't enough—not for the woman I married."

I waited, not wanting to pry but hoping he would continue with these confidences. My waiting silence seemed the best approach. I folded my hands and watched shadows flicker on the strong planes of his face.

He leaned forward, staring into the fire, as he rested his arms on his legs. "I haven't had Philippe very long—only a few months, in fact. His mother took him away when he was only two years old. She left me for a young prospector who hit a rich vein and was an overnight millionaire. They must have lived it up for several years until he lost control of his mine or made some poor investments. Anyway, he must have dumped her and she eventually left Philippe in the care of a questionable woman and took off with someone else. The woman wrote to me and I went and got him.''

''How . . . how could she do it, abandon him like that?'' No wonder he had built such a defense around himself!

''I don't know, but I'm sure it wasn't the first time she dumped him on some stranger. Marianne took Philippe away from me because she knew it was a way to hurt me, not because she really cared about the child. She must have filled his head with hatred. He won't have anything to do with me. He lies, cheats, steals . . .''

My eyes flickered to the glass cabinet. The amethyst stone was gone. I remembered his tense little hands clutching it.

''He hasn't had any schooling, can't even write his name. And these nightmares! They tear me apart! And there's nothing I can do about it.''

''Time . . . time is what he needs,'' I said softly. ''You can give him time. Philippe'll come around. I've seen it happen at school. You can't give up, or be impatient. Just keep offering love, and pretty soon he'll take it.''

''You make it sound so easy.''

''No, it's not easy. But then'' —I had to smile— ''I've been given the impression that Kipp Halstead is up to any challenge.''

He smiled back. "Maybe I have been too impatient. And now that you're here to help . . ."

It was the opening I needed to talk about Aunt Esther. "After I talk to the doctor tomorrow, I'll know how soon I can take my aunt back to Kansas."

His smile had disappeared. "She's better off here until she's herself again. SuLang is completely devoted to her and guards her like a jealous dog."

"Yes, I know. I understand her possessive devotion . . ."

"SuLang's like that. She develops a kind of fanatic devotion for some people, but others . . ." He shrugged. "She's indifferent to me, and she doesn't like Philippe—"

"Or me," I finished, remembering those biting cold eyes. I told Kipp how guilty she had made me feel. "She mailed the letters for my aunt, and is resentful that I didn't come right away. I wish now that I had."

"Don't put a mantle of guilt on your shoulders. None of this is your doing."

"There seems to be a consensus that I should leave," I said, my tone accusing. "You included."

"I was only thinking about your safety. I'm glad you're here, Allie, very glad." The soft ripple in his deep voice when he said my name made me apprehensive.

"Thank you once more for your hospitality. And now I must say good night."

I did not want to raise my eyes to his as he stood beside me, but I could not avoid being drawn into their smoldering dark depths. The tousled hair around his face begged to be touched and smoothed, and the slight curve of his lips taunted me. "Thank you for listening," he said softly, and his hands lightly touched my arms. Tantalizing fingertips stroked my flesh in tiny movements, and from these minute points of contact, fiery warmth surged through me.

"Please . . . I must go," I said in a choked voice.

"Yes . . ." he said huskily. But he didn't move, and neither did I. My lips remembered his kisses. I did not understand this bewildering need that made me stand there and raise my face to his.

"It's all right," he whispered. "Don't tremble so." He gave a deep sigh. He lowered his head and touched a light kiss to my hairline. Then he set me firmly away. "I agree, Allie." His lips quirked. "It's definitely time for you to go."

I turned and fled upstairs, knowing that running away wasn't going to do a bit of good. In the wild beating of my heart there was fear, bewilderment, and pain, but under all of that there was also joy and the promise of excitement. Every sensory bud burst with new awareness, like a tender branch on a young tree just coming into leaf.

6

FOOLISHLY, I felt like humming the next morning as I dressed in a navy merino skirt and white shirtwaist which was my usual attire for the classroom. My eyes seemed unusually bright, my cheeks flushed pink as I looked in the mirror and fastened my hair in rosette braids over my ears. Before leaving my room, I looked eagerly out the window. My room was on the side of the house overlooking the valley below. In every direction, wooded slopes rose above timberline to jagged peaks with snow still caught in deep cirques near their summits. The sky was a deep periwinkle blue, cloudless and soft with the texture of shimmering silk. I drew in the thin, high air and wondered if it was responsible for my heady feeling—or if the prospect of seeing Kipp this morning had anything to do with it.

SuLang was hovering around Aunt Esther as I entered, and had already given her her breakfast. I prayed Aunt Esther wouldn't go into the hysterical shrieking of yesterday when she saw me. She must be better, I thought as I approached her, for she was sitting in the rocker plying a crochet needle. I was encouraged until I saw that she was fashioning a pair of booties.

I spoke softly to her. "Good morning, Aunt Esther."

A sweet, vacant smile remained on her lips as she concentrated on her crocheting. I made some innocuous remarks about its being a nice day, but she did not look up at my voice or acknowledge my presence. Tears flooded the corners of my eyes. She was gone from me . . . in a world of her own. My effervescent feeling dissipated. "When does the doctor come?" I asked SuLang as evenly as I could.

"Morning . . . before noontime."

"Thank you, I'll come back then . . . and, SuLang, I appreciate your taking such good care of my aunt. I know that you love her very much—and so do I. She was like a mother to me, too." I gave her a smile but did not get one in return. "Sometime I would like to talk to you about my aunt's . . . accident."

"Not my fault!" Her eyes narrowed beyond their natural slant.

"No, of course not. I'm not trying to blame you—I just want to know what really happened at the hotel."

"Evil spirits—"

"I don't believe in ghosts and evil spirits," I said firmly with an edge of irritation. "Someone could have struck Aunt Esther . . . and maybe caused Uncle Benjamin's fall. Won't you help me find out who?"

I saw a flicker in her eyes that might have been fear. I waited, but she refused to answer.

My spirits suddenly leadened, I left the room. As I started down the stairs, I looked over the balustrade just as a tall, robust young man with sandy hair came out of the library. I stopped halfway down and he looked up at me. Immediately his freckled face registered surprise that bordered on embarrassment. For a moment I thought he was going to pretend he didn't see me. Did he think I was a lady friend of Kipp's who had spent the night?!

Hiding my own embarrassment, I came down the rest of the steps. "Good morning." I nodded with as much composure as I could manage under the circumstances.

"Good morning," he stammered. He was in his early twenties and a light mustache at his upper lip gave him the appearance of trying to look older. "I . . . I work for Mr. Halstead . . . he sent me after some papers." He waved them at me as if I were questioning his explanation. "I'm Jim Chadwick, but everybody calls me Chad."

I relaxed. He was as nervous as I was. "Glad to meet you, Chad. I'm Esther Lacey's niece."

He grinned and we both seemed relieved. He had a friendly manner, like country folk back home. Dressed in heavy trousers and a blue workshirt, he carried a cowboy hat in one hand. "I didn't know Esther and Ben had such pretty kin. I do handyman jobs around town . . . and they always treated me real nice. From Kansas, right?"

"A small town—" I began.

"Me too. Small town in Oklahoma. Came to Colorado to find my fortune. Heard there was gold in the Rockies just waiting for a farmboy's pick." His laugh was strained. "Found out soon enough that it took more money than I had to stick it out." His boyish freckled face lost its glow. "If Kipp hadn't hired me . . . Well, he knows what it's like to have a run of bad luck—his mine caving in the way it did, and all the trouble getting his smelter into operation." Then he clamped his mouth shut as if he had just realized he was gossiping about his boss. "Anyway, I'm glad to meet you."

"My pleasure," I said, and meant it. Chatting with someone who looked like homefolk put a friendly feeling in the air.

"I hope, Miss Lacey, that I may see you again. Perhaps I could see you to church tomorrow. Reverend Gilly will be here tomorrow. He's a circuit preacher—comes once a month to Glen Eyrie to hold services in our little community church." Then he flushed. "I don't suppose you'd want to go . . . just getting here and all."

"I think that would be very nice," I said impulsively. He was the first person who had tried to make me feel welcome.

He blinked as if he thought he had misunderstood my ready acceptance. Then he gave me a smile that seemed to go from one large ear to the other. "Tomorrow, then. I'll borrow a buggy. Maybe we could take a little ride up the gulch after services."

"We'll see," I hedged, not wanting to commit myself. Maybe Kipp would take me for a drive. I realized that I was already thinking much too much about being with him. I gave myself another lecture about getting my emotions under control, but I'm afraid I was only half-listening.

I walked down the hall with Chad and he left by the side entrance, which I saw opened into the hall by the small sitting room. There was no one there, nor at the table in the breakfast room. My disappointment mocked my new resolution about not thinking about Kipp.

I ignored the single plate set out on the table and followed tantalizing odors of coffee and bacon that wafted in from the kitchen. I made my way through a small butler's pantry to a large kitchen that was as merry and bright as the rest of the house was brooding and empty. A monstrous stove, newly blackened, with shining nickel-plated handles dominated one wall. Warmth radiated from a banked fire, and I realized then that my hands were cold from dressing in my unheated bedroom. This was the only room that was comfortably warm. The rest of the house was a cold, empty shell and a sharp contrast to this bright, sunny kitchen. Smoked hams and cured meat hung from hooks in a large, well-stocked pantry. An array of brightly colored jugs and bottles was filled with spices and dried fruit. Bottles of cooking wine were lined up on a shelf, and I knew then how Tooley achieved some of his delicious sauces. Everything was clean, organized, and I doubted if Tooley would permit anyone to invade his domain. He was banging pots and pans around in a merry fashion. Philippe sat at a long table by himself, his slim shoulders hunched over a bowl of oatmeal.

"May I join you?" I asked brightly.

His glower was less than inviting, but I remembered the soft, relaxed little face I had seen last night on his pillow. Somehow I had to get by his defenses to that vulnerable little boy.

Tooley gave me a grin that crinkled up his blue eyes. "Sure and I thought I was mistaken about having such a bonny lass in the house . . . but here ye are, looking as pretty as a yellow flower blooming in Killarney. Now, what would ye be liking for breakfast?"

"Do I smell coffee and bacon?"

"And biscuits in the warming closet," he finished with his merry laugh. "I knew ye weren't one of them gals that turn up their noses at breakfast."

"Not me. I was raised on a farm. Breakfast's the most important meal of the day." I glanced at Philippe's untouched oatmeal. "Wouldn't you like to join me?"

His answer was adamant. "I don't like teachers."

"Hmmm," I mused, taking a cup of hot coffee Tooley poured for me. "I never liked them much myself." I leaned toward Philippe. "You know what the girls call me at the school where I teach . . . when they think I can't hear them? Lazy Lacey!" I laughed, trying to coax a smile from him. "Don't you think that's a good name?"

"Lazy Lacey," chuckled Tooley, but the child only looked somberly pensive.

"They even sing a little chant, 'Miss Lazy Lacey puts ribbons on her lacies.' "

"And you don't get mad?" Philippe said in wonderment.

"Heavens, no. Do you think I should?"

He thought about it and then nodded solemnly. "Yes." What other answer could I have expected? His world was made up of anger and revenge and punishment.

"Well, I think it's funny," I insisted, and laughed again, hoping to see that tense little mouth join in, but he just stared at me in that unabashed way of children. He watched me eat my breakfast with such fascination that I offered him a biscuit dripping with a slab of home-made butter. His belligerent expression didn't change—but he took it.

" 'Tis a bonny lass, ye are," Tooley cackled as he kept my plate plied with food and my mug filled. He had given me a blue-patterned plate with matching cup and saucer. I saw the rest of the set in a lovely maple hutch, the kind with deep shelves which showed off the delicate Dresden china. I wondered if Kipp's mother had once sipped from these cups.

"Well, now, I think that should hold me until noon," I laughed as I slipped my napkin back in its ring. "I'll have to find something to do to work off a feast like that."

Philippe's strident voice broke in. "You said we'd go rock hunting!"

I'd completely forgotten to ask Kipp about it. I turned to Tooley. "Do you think his father would mind if we take a short walk looking for rock specimens?"

"So it's prospectors yer aiming to be . . . looking for gold nuggets lying around on the ground, no doubt." His merry eyes twinkled. "Well, now, I reckon a little hike on that hill behind the stables would do you both a bit of good."

"Does that sound all right, Philippe? Right after lunch, we'll go hunt some marvelous specimens for the cabinet—"

"I want to go now!"

"I'm sorry, Philippe," I said in a reasonable voice. "I have to see the doctor about my aunt when he comes this morning."

"You lied! You said you'd go—"

"I will, but not until this afternoon!"

"You won't . . . you won't! You're like all the others." He threw down the uneaten biscuit, pushed away from the table, and ran out of the back door.

"Philippe . . ." I tried to call him back, but the screen door only slammed behind him.

"Poor little lad," sighed Tooley. "Fighting and snapping like a frightened little stray. 'Tis a sad life he's had, dumped with this one and then another, and then his mother taking off and leaving him like that." He shook his round head. "Little wonder it's little faith he has in what people say."

"He seems to trust you, and that's a start," I told Tooley. "And I'll show him I mean what I say. As soon as the doctor leaves, I'll hunt him up for our hike."

90

" 'Tis a blessing for sure that you've come to this house."

Tooley's words put my spirits back on an optimistic track. I returned to my aunt's room to wait for the doctor. When he came, I learned that my optimism was ill-founded.

Dr. Walter Yates was a squat, balding man somewhere in his late fifties. His lined and puffy face bore the weathered scars of caring for humanity under miserable conditions. His eyes were kind and his touch gentle as he listened to Aunt Esther's heartbeat and looked into her pupils. Something remained in his manner of the young, idealistic physician he must have been at one time, before needless deaths, illnesses, and horrible injuries made a mockery of his skills.

"Can I take her back to Kansas? Is she well enough to travel?"

"That's a long, hard journey. Might be too much for her. Her heartbeat is irregular, but it might be just stress . . ."

He spoke softly to Aunt Esther and watched her eyes as they focused on some point just beyond him. Then she said quite plainly, "Benjamin . . . where's Benjamin? Will he be here soon?"

I closed my eyes as a sharp pain stabbed my heart.

The doctor sighed. "No change."

"I . . . I think she knew me last evening, briefly," I said in a tremulous voice. "And I'm sure she knew I was here in Glen Eyrie. She

91

became quite agitated, and screamed at me to go—as if she were trying to protect me."

The expression in his heavy-lidded eyes did not change, but I felt a quickening of interest. "She called you by name?"

"Yes. At first she talked to me like a child going off to school . . . but then, when I tried to make her understand that I had come here as she asked, she screamed, 'You must leave . . . go, Allison, go!'" I was close to tears, remembering. "What has happened to her? Is she ill physically? Or has her mind gone?"

"The blow on her head was severe, and I'm sure there's some loss of memory, but there's more. An emotional trauma has exacerbated the physical injury. Retreating into the past is a protective mechanism, when the horrors of the present are too great to be borne. The mind can break down too, you know, just like a horse loaded with one too many burdens."

"Will she . . . get better?"

He shrugged. "I don't know. The damage may have already been done. The death of her husband was a great blow, and yet, she kept on, trying to manage the hotel and fight a series of unfortunate happenings."

"What do you mean?"

"Some guests were frightened by shattering windows in the dead of night. A prospector fell down a flight of stairs . . . guests found their belongings destroyed. Word got out that it was haunted, a bad-luck place. She finally had to sell out."

A deep chill penetrated to the depths of my bones. *And Kipp had bought it!*

"Funny thing about your uncle's death. When they called me, the body still lay at the bottom of the ravine. Apparently he had been dumping trash over the edge . . . lost his balance and fell. They were doing some remodeling, you know, and he was taking wheelbarrows of dirt and refuse to this dumping spot. That was the funny thing. The wheelbarrow was still at the top of the cliff . . . but empty. Why didn't it go over with Ben when he lost his balance?"

The silence screamed an answer. *He was pushed!* I mouthed the horrible words and the doctor nodded. "That's what crossed my mind, too. And then, when your aunt was found unconscious . . ."

"Why didn't you do something . . . go to the authorities?"

He put a restraining hand on my shoulders. "This is a frontier town. The law is practically nonexistent. Besides, I had no evidence, only a feeling. Your uncle could have lost his balance and tumbled down the ravine. Your aunt could have had a dizzy spell and struck her head."

"But *you* don't think they were accidents!"

"I have my doubts, and that's what worries me. I think your aunt is right. You should leave here as soon as possible."

Everywhere I turned, I got the same advice. *Leave Glen Eyrie!* At the moment I was numbed by what the doctor had told me. Someone had a vicious vendetta against my aunt and uncle. Dr. Yates indicated that it might include me.

Could I turn heel and flee like a frightened rabbit? I thought not. My aunt seemed safe enough for the moment. I had to find some answers. I owed Esther and Benjamin that much. Whoever it was who had brought this tragedy upon them should be made to pay. We Laceys had always prided ourselves on being fighters—I would not run away!

After the doctor left, I stayed with my aunt until SuLang arrived with a lunch tray. The oppressive atmosphere in the house gave me good cause to be grateful for the outing I had planned with Philippe. I came down to the kitchen with bonnet and gloves and good walking shoes, ready to go rock hunting.

"Where's Philippe?" I asked Tooley.

The Irishman was flour up to his elbows, kneading sourdough bread. "Glory be! I knew ye meant what ye said. He's been gone all morning . . . but I set a sandwich out for him and I think he's eating out by the barn. Won't ye be needing a bite of lunch?"

My visit with the doctor had taken away my appetite. "I'm still full from breakfast," I assured him. "Maybe I'll have tea when I come back."

"There'll be bread fresh from the oven by then." He nodded. "Have yerself a nice walk."

An overhead sun spread a pristine brightness upon the high mountain terrain that made me grateful for the brim of my bonnet. I was glad I had decided against bringing a shawl, for the warm sunlight eased away the chill left by dark halls and unused rooms in the house. The stable and other outbuildings were located across a small clearing, and as I crossed it, the earthy smells of a barnyard and stable greeted my nostrils.

"Philippe," I called as I reached the open door of the stable.

"He not here." The Oriental man who had met us upon our arrival emerged from the darkness of the barn. Ching Lee, SuLang's brother. He must have been currying a horse, for he held a currycomb in his hand and it was full of sorrel hair. "Boy not here." His resemblance to SuLang was unmistakable, but his expression was much softer—and friendlier. Maybe he would be willing to talk to me sometime.

'Thank you. We were supposed to go for a hike, and Tooley said he was eating a sandwich out here."

He nodded, his long black queue bouncing. "He eat, and then go." He pointed in the direction of a band of thick conifer and aspen trees. "Maybe go fishing in creek."

"Yes, thank you, I'll walk that way. Maybe I'll catch up with him."

Apparently Philippe wasn't over his little tantrum. Well, I would take a walk without him. Maybe if he saw me, he would realize that I meant what I said and we could come back and hunt rocks behind the barn. I left the clearing and took what seemed to be a path of sorts through a forested area west of the house. I had no intention of walking along the edge of the promontory with its sheer cliffs. A creek must lie in the direction that Ching Lee had pointed.

I would find it and sit on a mossy bank and sort through my heavy thoughts.

Once under the canopy of thick trees, I realized I should have brought my shawl. The warmth of the sun did not penetrate through needled branches. The air was dank and smelled of wet earth and decaying leaves. An infinity of trees stretched around me in every direction, and the path I followed through them was uncertain, at times disappearing completely. No aspen trees with their white bark grew here; only tall ponderosas with rough layered bark fought with Douglas fir trees for space. The conifers massed together, challenging me to walk between them. Above me, long needles on curved branches vibrated softly like the strings of a mournful instrument. Looking up, I saw that only the tips of the trees shone silken in the sunlight.

The things the doctor had told me weighed so heavily on my mind that I just kept walking, expecting to come back into the sunshine at any moment. Deadfall on the forest ground crackled and snapped under my feet. Mosses and lichens coated tree trunks, rocks, and logs in the dark interior, and a musty fungus scent overpowered the crisp pine smell that came from sap beading on the trees. This slow, laborious walk was nothing like the easy stroll I had imagined. A sense of uneasiness settled upon me. I don't know what made me stop abruptly and swing around. Maybe a sixth sense told me I was being watched or followed. I caught the glimpse of a small face peering at me from behind some wild bushes.

"Philippe," I said, and then laughed in relief. He had been following me every step of the way. "Hello, I was hoping I'd find you. Come on, let's go find some rocks."

But even as I spoke, he darted ahead. I could see him bounding around tree trunks and hopping over fallen logs just ahead of me.

I laughed, gathered my skirts, and bounded after him. I was young and healthy and ready to enjoy a game of chase. At first my feet flew nimbly over the needled ground. However, the high altitude quickly took its toll. Soon I panted and slowed to a walk. The terrain grew more rugged. The uneven ground threatened to twist an ankle; broken branches snagged my clothing and snatched viciously at my hair and eyes. I had lost my enjoyment of the chase, and I did not want to be abandoned in this dark woods.

"Philippe, come back here." I used my schoolmistress tone, but he ignored it. I was relieved that he stayed within sight, turning his head and giving me what might have been a laugh, coaxing me like a Pied Piper through the woods.

"Philippe! Wait . . . Philippe, come back here."

Suddenly he was gone! I couldn't see him . . . and he didn't answer. A sudden panic drove me forward. "Philippe!"

Where was he? I stopped and searched for some sign of him peeking at me. Had he deliberately led me here to lose me in the forest? I should have been prepared for such a trick.

Then I saw him, just ahead where the trees thinned, and I saw a splash of bright sunlight.

Relieved and ashamed that I had doubted him, I plunged out of the band of trees—and then stopped in terror! Just ahead of me the earth ended! I tottered on the edge of a precipice. Instant vertigo engulfed me. Before I could spin around, I had the distinct impression of a sudden pressure on my back.

I lost my balance! My scream filled the air as I went over.

7

AS I fell, my full skirts billowed out. I felt a sudden jerk and heard the sound of tearing cloth. Somehow, miraculously, my skirt and petticoat had caught on a dwarf cedar tree growing out of the rocks. Its thick branches held my skirt and petticoat like a hanger. The fabric ripped from my weight but it slowed my fall enough to allow my feet and hands to gain purchase on a small ledge a few feet below. I could not believe the miracle as I sprawled on the narrow shelf of limestone. I didn't move, not only because the fall knocked the wind out of me but also because raw terror kept me paralyzed. I feared the slightest movement would send me over the edge, and prayed that it would not give way with my weight.

My senses could not take in what had happened. One minute I had been in the forest, the next tottering on the rim of a chasm. I'd had no warning that the thick band of trees hugged the edge of a precipice. Emerging suddenly from the dark forest into the bright sunlight had

brought a moment of blindness. And then . . . ?
I tried to recall that last sensation of being
pushed. I could not be sure. Perhaps my own
phobia of heights had caused the illusion.

Philippe—where was Philippe?

I closed my eyes against a thought that twisted
like a knife. Had he led me through the woods
to this rocky ledge—and then shoved me over?
He had been angry with me—but no, it couldn't
be. And yet, a moment before, I had feared he
was deceitfully leading me into the forest to
lose me. I knew he was a disturbed child, filled
with angry emotions, aggressive and resentful.
But I couldn't think anything so horrid of a
seven-year-old boy! I clenched my eyes shut.
The truth was, I had come upon the edge of the
precipice so quickly that I lost my balance—and
yet the impression of that sudden pressure on
my back haunted me. If not Philippe, who?
Who could have known I was going to lurch
out of the woods at this spot—unless someone
had heard me calling and thrashing through the
undergrowth! My mind wouldn't function. I
couldn't find my way through the terrifying maze
of what had happened. I only knew that it was
a miracle I was still alive.

"Philippe . . . Philippe . . ." I called.

No answer.

Only wind humming through the nearby trees
broke the deathly stillness. Sobs crowded up in
my throat. He wasn't going to come. And then
there was a sudden swish of bird wings. A
huge eagle circled within feet of where I lay.
Glen Eyrie . . . the glen of eagles. He must

100

have a nest somewhere near in the rocks. I had heard of the big birds plucking out the eyes of helpless prey. Fresh terror spurted into my already overloaded system.

I moved and dislodged a piece of loose rock. It went over the edge and I heard it hit far below. If the ledge on which I lay gave way . . . I did not know how far I was from the house, but I feared hysterical calling would only use up my energy. I must sit up and see if I could possibly pull myself back up on solid ground— and all of this must be done without looking down, I told myself. I had never been good at heights; in childhood I was always the last one to jump out of the barn onto the hayrack.

The eagle increased his circle, allowing his wide wingspan to float darkly against the sky. He wove a mesmerizing pattern and I jerked my eyes away from the soaring bird.

Slowly I lifted my head. I loooked over the edge in spite of myself. A sudden dizziness threatened to pull me over the side. I cried and threw out my hands to grab the scraggly, deformed tree that had saved my life. A solitary spot of green in the plunging cliff, it was growing in a narrow crevice and its roots had good purchase. As I sat there clutching the twisted branches, I saw my plight. I was marooned on a piece of narrow stone not much longer than my body. There was open space all around me except on one side, where a sheer wall rose too high for me to climb. My hope that I could stand up and pull myself back up onto solid ground was folly. My arms would not reach that high—and there was nothing to grasp in order to pull myself upward.

I closed my eyes and hugged the scratching cedar branches. Don't faint! Don't do anything foolish! Don't panic! My ears roared with a wild, lurching pulse and for a moment I thought I was imagining a rhythmic, humping sound. Then I jerked my head up.

The earth was vibrating. Horse's hooves!

I screamed. "Help . . . help!"

They came closer and closer.

"Help! Please help! Somebody help!" My good lungs were augmented by pure terror and my cries rose harshly to the unseen rider.

In another moment Kipp was looking down at me, astride a black horse.

"Kipp . . . Kipp . . ." I sobbed. My vision blurred with grateful tears. "Thank God," I sobbed.

"Allie! For Lord's sake, don't move."

It was such a needless order that I sobbed hysterically. Tears of joy poured down my face and I couldn't stop myself from blubbering. "I fell . . . my skirts caught . . ."

"It's all right," he soothed. "I've got a rope on my saddle. Just stay quiet, understand? Don't panic. Just stay still."

I nodded and managed a weak smile. "I'm not going anywhere."

In another minute a rope dangled in front of my face. "Put the loop around your waist," he ordered. "Slowly, that's it."

It took sheer will to let go of the tree with one hand and slip the loop around my waist.

"Good . . . now I've got you. You're safe. You're not going to fall." His deep voice was like a gentle stroking.

At that moment a warning crackling came from the tiny ledge.

"It's going to break," I screamed.

"Allie! Up on your feet!"

I sobbed, "I can't." The ledge was going to go out from under me at the slightest movement, I knew it. "I can't—"

"Yes, you can! Stand up! I've got the rope . . . you're safe, Allie. Stand up . . . facing the wall. You don't have to look down! Now, move!"

His commanding voice broke through my terror and I wavered to a sitting position.

"Let go of the branch. Grab the rope with both hands. And then stand up! Keep your hands tightly on the rope. I've tied it around the saddle horn, and when the horse moves back, I want you to start climbing up with your feet. You can do it. First lesson in mountain climbing," he said in a teasing tone at odds with his tense expression.

Letting go of that twisted branch was the hardest thing I ever had to do in my life. I accomplished it only by listening to Kipp's firm, reassuring voice.

I let go and grabbed the rope with both hands.

"Good! Now stand up."

The ledge gave a second threatening creak and I jerked up, wavering slightly but holding tightly to the rope looped around my waist.

"Are you ready?"

I managed a croaking "Yes."

The rope tightened. I held on and suddenly I was in a horizontal position with my feet moving up the wall. I don't remember how I did it, but I walked up that cliff! The next memory I have is of his firm arms going around me. My body shook with tremors that sent my teeth chattering. I couldn't fight a rising hysteria that made me talk and cry and sob all in the same breath. I put a scissors hold around his neck as if he were the only firm object on the face of the earth.

"Easy . . . easy . . . that was a good job. You walked up the face of that cliff like a professional. Maybe you're a born mountain climber."

That statement was so far from the truth that I had to laugh. The world was slowly coming back into focus.

"That's better."

I managed to loosen my arms from around his neck. I was on solid ground, I reasoned. The earth was not going to give way under me. The silent lecture did some good, but the sensation of falling still stayed with me. I knew that terrifying moment of hurtling over the edge into vacant air would be with me always. I shuddered. He kept me close as he reached into his saddlebag and brought out a small flask.

"All mountain climbers need a drink after a successful assault," he continued to tease, and I was grateful for his manner. I knew he was trying to put my narrow escape in a different perspective. I choked as he put the bottle to my lips and tipped the fiery liquid into my mouth. Its warmth radiated through my body and my shivers eased away. I had never had a drink of hard liquor before coming to Glen Eyrie. If this kept up, I could turn into a real tipper, I thought.

"There . . . that's better. It's all over."

I knew it was, but my knees were still too weak to hold me. Only his firm arms kept me from slumping to the ground.

"Are you hurt? Did you break something?"

"N-n-no." My teeth were still chattering.

"Thank God."

He guided me away from the precipice and eased me down on the needled ground under a tall pine. The shock of what had happened to me began to ease away and my breathing and heartbeat returned to a somewhat normal rate. He let me take my time and handle the shock in my own way. One arm circled me protectively and I closed my eyes and leaned back against the cleft of his shoulder. My skirt and petticoat hung in jagged tears and I was covered with powdery red dirt. My bonnet hung by its streamers halfway down my back and my hair straggled loosely around my face. But I didn't care. For the moment all that mattered was that he was here, and I was safe. I would think about something as mundane as my appearance later.

He was bareheaded and dressed in workclothes, as if he'd been doing manual labor. The debonair, cane-twirling gentleman was gone.

As if he read my thoughts, he said, "I've been up at the smelter site, trying to give the workmen a hand. I came back for lunch and . . ." His eyes clouded and then he tipped the flask and took a deep swig as if his own nerves needed settling. Then he held it out to me. "Another one?"

I hesitated. Every bone in my body was beginning to ache. "Maybe a sip." His eyes softened as he handed it to me. "I like a woman who can hold her liquor." His tone was light but his expression was still somber and concerned. "Are you ready to tell me what happened, Allie?"

It was a simple question, but my mind reeled. What had happened? Could I honestly say that his son had led me to the precipice and pushed me over? How could I voice such vicious suspicions? Such talk would only put additional strain on the problems between them. I did not want to be the cause of a worsening relationship. I must be absolutely sure before I said anything. "I . . . I was taking a walk," I answered vaguely. *Had Philippe deliberately led me to this spot?* "How did you find me?" I had a legion of questions of my own that I wanted answered.

"A walk! What on earth were you doing walking along a dangerous precipice like this? Tooley said you'd gone rock hunting behind the barn. Then Philippe came running back to the house just as I arrived, sobbing that he heard you scream . . . but he didn't know what had happened to you."

It could have happened that way, I thought. The memory was suddenly less clear than before. Had that pressure on my back been only my imagination? Maybe I had just lost my balance—like my uncle!

My face must have reflected a spurt of inner terror. He took my hands and held them tightly. "What is it, Allie? Tell me."

"This morning, the doctor said he wasn't certain my uncle was killed by the fall. He thought he might have been struck and killed before—"

"Good Lord!" Kipp swore. "I don't understand. At the time, Doc Yates seemed satisfied that it was an accident. Why didn't he say something then?"

"He wasn't sure. There's no way to prove it."

Kipp was silent, and suddenly I felt dark rumblings coming from him. He was not my compassionate rescuer. All the horrible things that had happened at the hotel, which had forced my aunt to lose it, seemed to benefit only one person—Kipp Halstead. And too many people didn't want me here—and I had ignored their warning. I took my hands away from his, and his soft expression hardened.

"What's the matter? Your eyes give you away, you know. What dire thoughts are you having about me now?"

I couldn't answer.

"I see. Well, it's obvious I'm not high on your list of confidants. You don't trust me, do you?"

I turned my head away but he wouldn't let me evade the question. With a firm hand he cupped my chin and forced me to look deep into those blue-gray eyes. "Answer me."

The harshness of his tone made me gasp, "No . . ."

He dropped his hand. His eyes shuttered and I couldn't tell if it was pain or anger that had flickered there for an instant. He gave me his practiced smile. "Well, perhaps it's for the better. You're much too vulnerable. Come on, let's get you back." He stood up. "Can you walk?"

I nodded, but before I knew what was happening, he had swung me up into his arms, carried me to his horse, and set me in the saddle.

He took the reins and led the horse in a brisk gait. Sunlight made his hair blue-black like a raven's wing, and the rippling muscles of his back and thighs brought a tightening in my chest. I had never experienced this devastating whirlwind of emotions. Even though I was half-frightened of him, I wanted to touch him . . . feel his arms around me . . . and raise my lips to that firm yet mobile mouth. When his eyes washed over me, I wanted to sink in their depths. He was right: I was vulnerable and I must strengthen my defenses against him. I must not let my emotions get in the way. I must keep a distance between us. He had saved my life, but there were too many murky depths to his nature—and his son's—to let my guard down.

As we reached the clearing with Kipp leading the horse, Tooley came loping toward us on his bandy little legs. "The saints be with us!" he swore. "Sure and 'tis a fright ye gave this poor old heart, lass."

"She fell," Kipp said briskly, "but it's all over now."

His words were hollow and mocking. Nothing was over. As the dark, cold house welcomed me back, perhaps I sensed that things had just begun.

8

I did not sleep well that night. My dreams were filled with golden eagles swooping at me, their clawed talons and large curved beaks raking my face. They came in hordes and I could not get away from them. I stepped backward over a ledge—and woke up with my heart racing and my breath caught in my throat. I did not know if I had cried aloud or not, but no one came. My pillow was moist from sweat and I lay there a long time, afraid to go back to sleep.

The next morning, I awoke with a groan. My bruised body protested every movement. The world swept back upon me. My head ached and my mind refused to wrestle with doubts and suspicions. I had stayed in my room the remainder of the day after my ordeal, resting and sleeping fitfully. SuLang had brought me a tray for my evening meal and I had not protested this cosseting.

It would have been easy to play the invalid but I knew that I must not give in to depression and doubt. "A foe faced is a foe vanquished," was one of Miss Purcell's homilies and it seemed appropriate this morning. Then I remembered with a start that it was Sunday morning, and I had promised Chad to go to church with him. At the school, worship services had been held in a small chapel on the grounds and attendance was required of all staff. It would be a pleasant change to attend church without a parcel of giggling girls to supervise.

As I dressed, I wondered if anyone else in the house would be going. Then I laughed at myself. Despite all the firm scolding I had given myself, what really sent my pulse racing was the thought of Kipp sitting beside me, dressed in his Sunday best, singing in that deep, resonant voice of his.

But the fantasy was just that—Kipp was not in the house and Tooley was evasive about his whereabouts. He probably had not come home last night, I thought with a peculiar stab of pain. Philippe kept out of my sight, and my determination to talk to him about yesterday was thwarted.

Aunt Esther was her listless self, just sitting and staring in her rocking chair, not even plying her crochet needle. She even seemed unresponsive to SuLang's administrations as the Oriental woman brushed and braided her thin gray hair. My heart ached with sadness, and a feeling of helplessness sent my spirits plummeting further. I was grateful to Chad for giving me the chance to escape the oppressive house for a few hours.

He helped me into the rented hack rather clumsily and I couldn't help but compare his lack of grace with Kipp's smooth and polished manners. Then I chided myself for the comparison, for I knew how that savoir faire had been achieved. Kipp's absence from the house was testimony to his rakish activities. I wondered if he had decided to visit Millie's establishment and get acquainted with the new "boarders." The memory of the two women on the train came back and I wondered once more about the mystery lady. Was she a special attraction brought up from Denver City for more discriminating tastes? For men like Kipp Halstead perhaps? As usual, my imagination ran away with me. I chided myself and tried to concentrate on enjoying this outing.

I was not unaware of the admiration in Chad's hazel eyes as he surveyed my pastel blue-and-green lawn dress. I wore a straw bonnet with silk flowers and velvet streamers which I had purchased for my trip. With feminine satisfaction, I knew that I need make no apology for my appearance. Somehow that knowledge bolstered my confidence about meeting new people in this alien setting.

I held on to the hard seat as we came down the steep, circuitous road that doubled back on itself a dozen times before we reached the bottom. Even in bright daylight the narrow passage looked treacherous. I wondered how on earth any vehicle navigated the road in wintertime. We passed Lucretia's house about halfway down.

I couldn't keep myself from peering at it, searching for any sign that Kipp was there.

Chad noticed my scrutiny and with a knowing nod pointed out a bridle path coming down the bluff from Kipp's house, and for a moment my heart stopped as I followed it upward. *It came out close to the promontory where I had fallen yesterday!* I closed my eyes as my stomach took a sickening dip.

"What's the matter? Don't be worrying about going off the edge . . . I know these roads are kind of scary until you get used to them . . . I remember how it was when I first came out here from Oklahoma. I wanted to crawl up some of the trails on my hands and knees." He laughed and I gave him a weak grin in return. I would think about the path and its implications later.

Chad was a good conversationalist and chatted with me without any pretenses. He pointed out houses built nearly on top of each other and chuckled. "There's a saying around here that a fellow can spit tobacco off his front porch and put out the fire in his neighbor's chimney."

I laughed appreciatively and took a deep breath of crisp air. The cloudless heavens looked translucent in a wash of deep blue. As the hack's wooden wheels rose and fell in the rutted rod, I let my eyes travel in every direction. The scene changed dramatically from the valley floor, upward through bands of thick forests to rocky cliffs and then stretching upward above timberline to snow-tipped mountain ridges. There was beauty here, but treachery too, as if nature laughed at man's feeble efforts to control her . . . perhaps maliciously playing a joke on his greed and only waiting to reclaim the landscape once more for herself.

"That's Harrigan's Gulch, up that way," said Chad, pointing up a ravine. "First strike was made there by an Irishman, Sam Harrigan, and he's responsible for Glen Eyrie's poetic name. Several attempts have been made to change it, but the name has stuck. Lots of money was taken out of these hills in the beginning. Nothing but a tent camp here for quite a while. You could pan gold out of the streams then, or make yourself a sluice or rocker and run the ore through it to filter out the gold." He shook his head sadly. "Hard-rock mining is taking over now. Good strikes are few and far between. Even the old established mines like Kipp's Goldstock mine have begun to play out. Then that freak rock slide closed him up. He's sinking everything he has in this new smelter."

"Are he and Lucretia Poole partners?" I pried, my curiosity overcoming my good manners.

"Not anymore. After her husband died, she sold her interest in the Goldstock to Kipp. Maybe she knew the vein was about to run thin. Anyway, she started investing her money in other businesses—banks, a sporting house which she's leased to Millie, and now a playhouse. That woman's making money hand over fist. It's Kipp who's watched his fortunes dry up."

Did he think a Victorian hotel and new smelter

might help recoup them? The thought rose unbidden and I swallowed against a bad taste rising in my mouth.

Chad pointed out a new building that housed a volunteer fire brigade. A shiny red wagon with dozens of buckets adorning its sides stood ready for use. Even on Sunday morning there was a raucous air about Glen Eyrie, I thought as we traversed through a labryinth of narrow streets. Even this early in the day, board sidewalks were crowded with men who might just be emerging from an all-night poker game, or perhaps were leftovers from a Saturday-night drunken brawl. A few women in calico dresses sat with children in the back of mule-drawn wagons. They looked dusty and hot, as if they had come a good distance to spend the day in town.

I heard the sound of a church bell above the clamor of horses and people as Chad maneuvered the spotted gray horse through a maze of lumbering wagons, buggies, carts, and horseback riders. The community church had been built on the opposite side of the town, high on another ridge. As Chad urged the horse and hack up yet another steep slope, I clung to the seat and despaired that there wasn't any flat land in this glen of eagles on which to build a decent town.

"Well, here we are."

It was a pleasant-looking building, I thought, with a peeled-log exterior softened by spruce and pine trees that scented the air with a brisk mountain fragrance. A plain cross adorned a modest bell tower and two graceful lancet windows flanked the front door, which stood open, waiting to receive Sunday worshipers.

The sanctuary was simple and unadorned, I saw as we took our seats. Wooden pews flanked a narrow aisle leading to a simple altar. Thumping chords from a small organ vibrated to the high ceiling with the tune of "Come Thou, Almighty King." The organist was a small, plump woman who bobbed her head in rhythm to her pumping feet, and I had to smother my urge to laugh as I watched her.

My eyes traveled to a gray-haired man sitting on a straight chair behind the pulpit. Dressed in black, his rawboned frame seemed to be all angles, sharp and straight. "Reverend Gilly, he's a circuit preacher, rides all over the mining camps," Chad whispered. Then my eyes fell to his feet and I saw that with his shiny black frock coat and trousers, he was wearing cowboy boots. I covered my lips to hide a smile.

The sermon was about what I had expected— the wages of sin, and the promise of deliverance to those who would mend their ways. The reverend's flock seemed to be composed mostly of women, squirming children, and a few elderly men. After the service, he stood at the door and shook each person's hand, calling everyone by name. He gave me a crooked smile that was full and hardy as Chad introduced me. "Glad to make your acquaintance . . . and how is your aunt?"

"The same, I'm afraid."

"She never missed a Sunday when she was well. I've been calling on her, and will look forward to seeing you. You'll be taking her back home, I suspect?"

"I don't know," I said honestly. Then I told him what the doctor had said about her weak heart and that the journey might be too much for her.

"Sorry to hear that. I'll keep her in my prayers. And I hope we can look forward to seeing you often at services." He patted my shoulder and then turned to greet the next in line.

I smiled randomly at several women clustered outside the church. My bonnet was getting its share of attention, and I intercepted several envious looks.

A small woman squinted at me from behind spectacles. Then she stepped up and introduced herself as Ellie Peters. "I used to sew for your aunt," she said in a friendly tone. Her forehead was puckered as if she habitually threaded a needle in dim light. "I'm sorry to hear she's poorly. Please give her my best."

Chad helped me into the hack and then took a different route away from the church as he suggested a short ride up the canyon. I didn't admit it to myself, but I wanted to go back and see if Kipp had returned. Rationalizing that I didn't care where he was or what he was doing, I smiled at Chad and said that would be nice. After all, Chad was good company and I was lucky to have a new friend in this horrible place. This made me think of Emmett and I deter-

mined that I would write to him this afternoon
and describe Glen Eyrie as best I could.

This thought was put from my mind the next
instant as I became aware of the surroundings.
The street we were on was not one a lady
would ever describe to a man. It was obvious
that a cluster of small quarters belonged to ladies of the night. Several women lounged in
doorways, wearing scant dresses with low décol-
letage.

Chad gave the horse a quick flip of the whip
and I knew he was trying to leave this section
of town as quickly as possible. A large house
with draped windows caught my eye and I
almost had the courage to ask if it was Millie's
place, but managed to keep a rein on my curiosity. I could not, however, keep my eyes from
darting to see if Kipp's black horse or well-
sprung buggy was in sight.

At that moment a woman came out of the
front door and my breath caught in recognition.
It was the same brassy blond woman who had
been at the train depot. Dressed in a burgundy
brocade dress, she stared back at me boldly
from under the brim of a large hat. Why did I
have the feeling she knew exactly who I was? I
glimpsed the knowing smile on her face and
jerked my gaze back to the road. *Maybe she knew
exactly where Kipp was!*

"That's the Old Nellie mine over there, first
strike in these hills." Chad pointed to a gaping
black hole near the crest of a rocky incline.
"Was worth a fortune when Harrigan filed his

claim. Played out now, though." Suddenly there was a ragged edge to his voice. "I got here too late . . . all those stories about gold lying around on the ground were nothing but lies. Don't know how I'm going to go home. My folks sold off a section of land to grubstake me, and I lost it all!"

"I'm sorry," I murmured.

"I'm not licked yet. I'm not the simple farmboy I was when I came here. Learned a lot of things, and I'm aiming to change my luck."

The hillsides were littered with abandoned sluices and other weird structures which Chad told me were windlasses and rockers. When the gold rush was at its height, he said, these crevices had teemed with men and the sound of their picks and shovels, but now the wealth was settled in a few hands and the lone prospector could not compete with rising companies. I thought the hillside resembled a graveyard of sorts; hundreds of broken dreams were buried there. Greed brought its own price, and I wondered about people like Lucretia, Kipp, my aunt and uncle, and now even Chad, who refused to give up at any cost. As if to match my thoughts, the sun went behind a bank of gray clouds and I heard the rolling rumble of distant thunder.

"Looks like rain." Chad nodded, following my glance. "Better head back. It can come down quick and strong—like somebody emptying out a giant bucket from the sky. A cloudburst can send angry floodwaters down these washes in just minutes." He snapped the whip over the horse's rump and sent the hack jolting over deep ruts and fallen rocks.

When we returned to the house, he hurried me up on the porch. Twirling his hat, he said shyly, "There's a square dance planned to raise money for the volunteer fire brigade. Lots of fiddle music and good food. Would you like to go with me?"

For a second I entertained some foolish hope that Kipp might ask me to go. I hesitated and then chided myself. If I waited for him to ask me, I might sit at home all evening in this horrid house while he squired someone like Lucretia around. "I'd love to. We have toe-tapping square dances at home. Thank you for asking me."

He scurried away, hoping to get the rented horse back to the stable before the storm broke.

When I entered the house I hoped that Kipp had returned and might be in the library reading, or perhaps even waiting for me. My expectations were foolish. The library was dark, and cold, and empty. No fire had been laid in the grate. I berated myself for the wash of disappointment that made my steps leaden as I climbed the stairs to my room.

Thunder and flashes of jagged lightning heralded a downpour which Chad had described. The windows of my room became opaque with sheets of rain that pounded against the house. The wind moaned and shrieked like a crazed creature trying to get in. As I heard the rattling of the house, I worried the fierce downpour was violent enough to sweep it right off its foundation. I knew it was perched on the edge of a sheer cliff and all the terror of my accident the day before swept back in foolish proportions. I could almost feel the floor of my bedroom slipping away under my feet! I threw myself on the bed and covered up my head with a pillow in a childish manner—but it didn't help. Then a sharp crash of thunder brought me up. Lightning struck on the hill behind the house. Instantly another fork of lightning lit up the room, followed by a deafening thunder peal.. I lurched across the room and out into the hall.

I fled to my aunt's room, where I found her taking a nap. She was fully dressed, with a light cover over her thin body. Streaks of lightning and booming thunder near the house failed to disturb her peaceful sleep. I sat down in a chair beside her bed and drew comfort from her presence as I had done as a child. We had bad storms in Kansas, and many times we had fled into a cellar when a dark funnel cloud had been sighted on the horizon. She had always reassured me and made light of any danger.

Mellow light from a flickering lamp on the bedstead encased us in a protective circle, and memories of the past eased my taut nerves. I wished I could talk to her, pour out my bewilderment, ask her if she thought a malicious little boy had given me a deliberate shove over the cliff—or if it could have been someone else. Had someone bribed him to bring me to that spot . . . or had the whole thing been happenstance? Once more I questioned whether or not I had just lost my footing. Terror had erased any firm recall about that split second when I dashed out of the band of trees to find myself on the edge of a precipice. I wanted to tell her how Kipp had rescued me. If only I could talk to Aunt Esther about these bewildering feelings I had for a man who could hold me gently in his arms one minute, then react with building black rage the next. His moods could be light and flirtatious or darkly withdrawn and brooding. Had my aunt willingly accepted his hospitality—or had she been too ill to object? Was fear a part of her lucid moments because she knew where she was—and what had really happened to her and Uncle Benjamin?

As I sat there waiting for the storm to pass, the rumbling darkness outside matched my turbulent emotions. Finally the room began to lighten and the thunder became more distant. Spears of bright sunshine shot through glistening wet branches. I moved to the window and watched some indignant jays fan their electric-blue wings, cawing in a disgruntled manner as they dried them in the sun. I laughed at their antics and my inner storm eased away.

SuLang brought in Aunt Esther's lunch a few moments later. When I said I would eat with my aunt if she would kindly bring me a similar tray, she hesitated. My aunt's eyes were open and SuLang spoke softly to her as she coaxed her from the bed. Both of us were tense, waiting to see what Aunt Esther would do when she saw me. Since that first day, she had not shown any reaction, violent or otherwise, to my presence.

Her eyes seemed clear as she took a chair by a small table set in a small alcove. I quickly took a chair opposite her. "I'm going to have lunch with you, Aunt Esther," I said brightly. "Look . . . we've had a little rain. Everything's so bright and clean." I drew back the lace curtain so she could see.

A slight smile curved her lips as a blue jay swooped near the pane from a nearby needled branch. "Barn swallows," she said in a clear voice. "You must go and see if they've come back to their nest under the eaves." She looked me directly in the face. "And don't let the cat at them." Then her forehead furrowed. "Where is that scamp? Where is Tabby?"

Tabby had been dead for seventeen years!

"Where is he?" Her voice rose in a pitiful wail. "I want Tabby."

SuLang moved quickly on slippered feet to her side. She murmured to my aunt like one soothing a child about a lost toy, but the darting black looks she sent me could have cut diamonds. She blamed me for this lapse into the past. The girl coaxed some hot broth into Aunt Esther's mouth. Like a youngster whose attention has been diverted, my aunt's expression smoothed and she began to nibble on a slice of bread and jam.

My hopes of coaxing my aunt back into some kind of rational thought seemed doomed. Either the blow she had received on the head or her emotional trauma kept her from relating to the present. Any secrets she had were beyond reach. How could I find out who had harmed her and perhaps killed Uncle Benjamin, and now vented a twisted malevolence upon me? My presence only seemed to cause her to regress to those years before they left Hartford. And if I could bring her back to the present, could I live with the answers that I might find?

9

KIPP was at the breakfast table when I went
downstairs the next morning. I had heard horse's
hooves go past my window last evening while I
was still awake—somewhere around ten o'clock,
I thought. A few minutes later, I heard him
mount the stairs and pause a moment at the
top. My lamp was still flickering, for I had just
put down my book, and I wondered if he might
see that I was still awake. My heart thumped
fiercely as I held my breath. Then I heard his
retreating steps and the sound of his door closing. I scooted from the bed and made certain
the latch was turned on my door.

He had been gone from the house since Saturday night. Obviously he found other company more enjoyable than mine. I flounced over
to the bed and told myself I didn't care and that
the foolish tears that spilled hotly into my eyes
had nothing to do with him. Even if he had
come to my room to inquire about my well-
being, I would have haughtily kept my door
closed against him, I told myself. If only Aunt

Esther were well enough, we would move from this house and find other lodgings . . . and if I never saw Kipp Halstead again, it would be soon enough! I hated him, and his horrid house, and his insufferable handsome charm! I wanted to go back to Kansas, where life was predictable. I made a new vow to write to Emmett the first thing tomorrow and tell him how much I missed him.

The next morning I sailed into the breakfast room with my head high. But all my rationalizations about being immune to his devilish charm quickly went by the board. My breath quickened as he stood up and held a chair out for me.

"Good morning, Allison."

Allison! It wasn't "Allie" this morning.

"Good morning . . . sir," I said, a little piqued at his formal tone. One minute he was holding me in his arms offering me sips of brandy, and the next greeting me as if we had barely met. What a maddening, unpredictable person he was!

"And how are you feeling this morning?" His manner was solicitous, but I found it rather false. After all, I hadn't seen him since he sent me to my room to rest after my harrowing experience.

"Fine, thank you."

"Are you ready now to explain exactly what happened on the cliff?" He sat down and put his elbows casually on the table as he leaned toward me, searching my face, ready to evaluate my response.

I hadn't had the chance to talk to Philippe yet. I bit my lip. Did he already suspect his son and plan to deal severely with the boy? It seemed to me he was waiting for one word of confirmation from me that Philippe was at fault. No, I must keep my counsel. With my eyes lowered, I mumbled something about heights and the way they affected me. "I don't know what there is to say. I must have lost my balance." My voice trailed off and I knew from the set of that mobile mouth that he was angry with me.

"I see. How can I protect you if you're not honest with me?" he asked curtly.

"I . . . I don't know what happened," I said firmly. "When I do, I'll tell you."

"If it's not too late! Well, you don't seem any the worse for your adventure. I expected that you would spend yesterday resting. Obviously, I was mistaken. Did you enjoy your outing with young Chadwick?" His mocking tone put me on the defensive.

"Very much." I firmed my chin. "I enjoyed the service and had a pleasant ride up the canyon." Had someone told him, or had he seen us from Lucretia's place or Millie's? "I found it all very interesting."

"You didn't get caught in that storm, did you?"

I had to smother a smile. His tone was that of a father concerned that I might have been caught in a compromising situation. "No. We saw the dark clouds in time." Then impishly I asked, "Did you get caught in the rain?"

His eyes met mine in surprise; then he grinned.

"Touché. I might as well admit that I intended to be the one to show you around."

"Oh, there's plenty I haven't seen," I said boldly.

"Do you ride?" he asked as he served me a plate of eggs and ham kept warming on a sideboard.

"I'm a farmgirl, remember? Do you have some cows you want brought in?"

He laughed, and like quicksilver his mood changed. He put on his debonair manner. "No, but I imagine you would enjoy horseback riding. I have a mount in the stable that would suit you, I think. Marianne's sidesaddle is still around somewhere; she never did much riding. I'll tell Ching Lee to hunt it up. You should be safer wandering around on a reliable horse than walking through forests and plunging off cliffs." The last was said in a light manner, but he suddenly reached out and touched my hand. "You will be careful?"

"Yes. And thank you."

"Perhaps later in the week we could ride together."

All my determination to separate myself from him and his affairs melted like frost under a warm sun. "I'll look forward to it."

"Then I must be on my way." He stood up and I saw he was wearing a corduroy jacket, trousers, and heavy boots. His shirt was open at the neck and I glimpsed a mat of dark hair. As always, his virile presence dominated my senses. I looked away, knowing heat was creeping up into my cheeks.

"We're going to install some equipment in the smelter this morning," he said. "Another few weeks and we'll be in business." A boyish eagerness was reflected in the bright glint in his eyes.

"I'm anxious to see it." There was no pretense in my remark. He had swept away my protective defenses. I wanted to share his happiness. When he smiled like that, I felt wonderfully like laughing, forgetting about everything but being in his company.

"By the way," he said, responding to my smile. "I was wondering if you could spend some time with Philippe. His school attendance has been so fragmented that I fear he's quite illiterate."

"Of course. I'd be grateful to have something to do. I'm afraid that Aunt Esther is oblivious of my company."

He looked down at me and for a moment I thought he was going to lean over and kiss me. Instead he squeezed my shoulder. "Don't give up . . . you're good medicine, Allie . . . for all of us." With that he turned, picked up his cane, and left the room, leaving me foundering in the wake of his compliment.

When I went back upstairs, I met SuLang just leaving with my aunt's breakfast tray. I made my voice bright. "Good morning. How is Aunt Esther today?"

"Good. Missy no upset her!"

"I'll try not to," I promised as I entered the room.

I found Aunt Esther standing by the window,

looking out. This surprised me and I wondered if I could get her to take a little exercise.

"Good morning, Aunt Esther," I said brightly. Gently I took her thin arm and coaxed her, "Let's take a little walk down the hall." She moved slowly and in shuffling steps, but I was encouraged. "Maybe tomorrow I'll take you all the way to my room."

Her tranquil expression did not change but she gave a faint laugh, as if responding to something amusing in her mind. I left her sitting in her chair, crocheting a second bootie. I was satisfied that she had accepted my company without any sign of her former agitation.

I spent the rest of the morning washing out some of my things and hanging them outside in the brisk warm breeze that had them dry in no time. I sat on the back stoop and ate an apple and drank a glass of milk for lunch as I watched Tooley pluck a couple of chickens. When I asked about Philippe, Tooley said he'd taken a bucket and gone frog hunting.

"Does he go off by himself like that often?"

Tooley nodded. "Poor lad. All tangled up inside, he is."

"Do you think that he might do something violent?" Like shoving me off the side of a cliff, I added silently.

Tooley matted his fuzzy eyebrows together and gave several rapid plucks on the chicken before he answered. "It's not for me to be saying, but any cornered animal will be striking out, even when the hand is a helping one." He peered at me with those bright blue eyes. "He was asking me some questions about ye . . . as if someone was feeding him some poisonous ideas about ye being here to hurt him."

"But that's horrible! Who would lie to him like that? Twist his thinking so viciously?"

"Don't be asking me. So many weird things going on—'tis enough to curdle a man's soul or drive him to drink." He gave me a wry grin.

I changed the subject and asked him the names of the mountains rising clear and crisp in the midday sun. One looked like a sleeping figure, and Tooley told me of an Indian superstition which said that the Great Spirit would come someday and awaken him. Then peace and happiness would reign. I couldn't help but wonder if the legend had taken into account man's lust for gold. There was a viciousness here that defied such a benign prophecy, I thought.

From this high bluff I could see Glen Eyrie as if looking through the wrong end of a telescope. It sprawled up the narrow ravine, which hardly seemed wide enough to accommodate a tumbling creek, let alone a whole town. The scene was a far cry from Hartford, laid out in neat blocks, but I had to admit it had a captivating charm of its own. I could see how one might succumb to its rugged grandeur . . . and to a man like Kipp Halstead, who dared to live in this high, rocky glen of eagles. A warm feeling that had nothing to do with the bright clear sky or brassy sun enveloped me as I thought of Kipp's promise to take me horseback riding.

Then, because I was basically an impatient

person, I couldn't wait. "It's a beautiful day," I murmured to Tooley, and then said in a casual tone, "Kipp said this morning that he was going to arrange for Ching Lee to ready a horse for me. I think I'll take a little ride."

"Don't ye be going far. The weather in these parts is as changeable as a lassie's favor," he warned. " 'Tis an afternoon rain we have most days."

"I won't go far," I promised, and hurried up to my room to change into the modest riding habit which was required by Miss Purcell for all female staff. We had to accompany our girls on horseback for recreational rides and to and from school functions, and proper attire was important. I was rather pleased with the way I looked in the long-waisted jacket with a narrow cut which emphasized my firm bust and small waist. The full navy skirt was caught up on one side to show patent-leather boots, and at my neck I tied a silk scarf in navy and white polka dots. A tall pearl-gray hat had a swath of sheer cloth circling the brim, which gave a jaunty air to the rather severe, mannish costume. I was glad I had thought to bring it in my trunk, for I wanted to look my best when I went riding with Kipp.

I stopped in the kitchen and got another apple, then hurried to the stable. I wondered if Kipp had spoken to Ching Lee about my mount, or if I was premature in my eagerness to ride.

I was not disappointed. Ching Lee nodded at my request and brought out a lovely palomino mare with flaxen tail and mane. She took the apple from my hand with a neat snatch and I laughed as she noisily chomped it down.

"What's her name?" I asked as I patted her neck.

"Fancy," said Ching Lee with obvious pride. Her coat glistened and I knew she'd had a vigorous currying.

"Nice name . . . suits her." Then out of curiosity I asked, "What's Mr. Halstead's black horse called?"

"Midnight."

Very appropriate, I decided, for both horse and master.

Ching Lee cinched up a new-looking saddle and led the mare to a mounting block. He grinned approvingly as I lightly put my left foot into the stirrup and sprang up into the seat. Fancy stamped her hooves and then moved sideways in a skittish motion, but responded to a gentle but firm pull on the bit. What a joy! The horses we had at the school were reliable, steady mounts that offered little challenge or excitement.

Fancy moved easily out of the stableyard. There was a small pasture on one side of the stable, so I circled it several times while we became acquainted, until both of us felt secure with the other. Then impulsively I reined her away from the house and headed for the bridle path that led down from the house to the valley floor below.

I reined her to a stop when I reached the spot where the path came up on the promontory

and saw that it was only a short distance from
the place where I had tumbled over the edge.
Perhaps I had to reassure myself that someone
could have come up that way and waited for
me to burst out of the trees. Yes, it could have
happened that way. Someone could have dismounted, walked a short distance, and waited
for me. Even in the bright sunlight, I shivered.
Had Philippe played Pied Piper to lead me to
this spot? It was a curdling thought to think
someone might be twisting the mind of a small
boy with such treachery.

Fancy danced as if she were used to going
down the bridle path, so I loosened the reins. I
found her to be surefooted enough to keep my
eyes away from the plunging hillside and let
her have her head. Before we had gone any
distance, another path joined the one going
downward. It took off in a northernly direction,
running level into a heavily forested area. Fancy
automatically swerved in that direction so I decided to follow it, curious to know where it led.
The mare tossed her head and moved forward
with an air of familiarity, as if she were used to
this path. I wondered then if Kipp had chosen
Fancy for me because she had been all over
these hills and could undoubtedly take me home
if I got lost.

As we made our way through a thickening
tunnel of trees and brush, only feeble light fell
in slivers through needled branches. It was indeed the Hansel-and-Gretal forest of my youth.
The world instantly darkened in a tunnel of
trees. A dense growth of spruce and Douglas fir

shut out the sun, allowing only muted, smudged light to penetrate the eerie green-black patina of the woods. Damp, earthy odors rose from decaying deadfall on the forest floor. Brown needles, moist dead leaves, and scattered cones emitted a pungent scent.

Dead trees and fallen logs thickened the undergrowth, looking stark and gray against the green lushness of living trees—a grim reminder of this struggle in nature for only the strongest and fittest to survive. Already new growth was being choked by aggressive older trees spreading their roots to capture the ground, and greedy branches to capture the sky.

Fancy's hooves echoed in the stillness. No birds flitted through the trees. It was a forest for fairy tales, dragons, and prehistoric beasts, I thought in a flight of fancy, trying to laugh at myself for suddenly feeling trapped in this infinity of dark tree trunks, as if it were a silent world from which I could never emerge.

Fancy was plunging boldly ahead and I was relieved to see the landscape lighten. I could hear the soft rushing of a stream now and suddenly we emerged into a lovely meadow. I almost didn't see the cabin nestled back in the trees, and if Fancy hadn't given a sudden spurt forward like someone arriving home, I would have missed it.

Then I remembered. That first night, when Kipp had brought me to his house, he had pointed in this direction and mentioned the cabin he had built when he first came to Glen Eyrie. I reined Fancy and looked at it. I wondered if he had built it himself, for the logs looked rough-hewn, and a stone fireplace was unevenly mortared. Approaching it, I decided to investigate and satisfy my curiosity. I tethered Fancy at a corral post at the back of the cabin.

I knew a stream must lie behind the thick thatches of grasses and reeds because I could hear the chortling, gurgling, rushing water. A stand of spring-green aspen trees lined the meadow, and I saw that the small meadow behind the cabin was lush with catkins, all feathery in their pale lucid green softness, and a variety of other plants in mottled greens and yellows which I could not identify. Someday I would like to come here, I thought, and sit in the grasses and enjoy this tiny spot of flatland caught like an emerald between the dark forested mountains.

As I came around the side of the cabin, some instinct aroused an uneasiness I could not quite define. Was there a pair of eyes fixed on me? The thick trees edging the meadow could have hidden an army of eyes and I wouldn't have been able to see any of them. Even the small windows of the cabin were opaque like blind eyes. I froze for a minute, trying to analyze the sensation that was causing my heart to leap loudly into my throat. I knew then that I had broken my promise to Kipp to be careful. I was alone, in the depth of this forest where no one could answer a cry for help. A rising panic seized me. I felt an urge to cry out or turn, and I could do neither! My hands were clammy under my gloves, and yet warm sweat beaded on my brow under the brim of my hat.

The snap of a twig somewhere in the trees behind me brought an involuntary cry to my lips. The sound confirmed what I already sensed: someone in the darkness of the woods was watching me. I bolted up a front step and lurched into the cabin as if some mad Furies were after me. I slammed the door shut and leaned against it, breathing heavily.

I don't know how long I stood there trying to still a rising sense of panic. Who was it hiding and watching? Finally I eased over to the small window and peered out, but only possessive black shadows under the thick grid of branches met my eyes. The scene was benign. A tiny ground squirrel darted across the ground, mocking the terror that had risen in my chest.

I had let my imagination run away from me again! I gave a shaky laugh. Undoubtedly some wild rodent had snapped a branch and I had given way to a play of nerves. My breathing began to return to normal. I looked about the room spanning the front of the cabin and realized with a start that it was clean and comfortably furnished in crude but functional furniture. A stuffed chair was pulled up to the stone fireplace, which held the hint of a recent fire. I walked toward it and my eyes fastened on a nearby table. Mark Twain's new novel, *Innocents Abroad*, lay there. The one I had seen in the library—with the bookmark in a different place!

This is where Kipp was Saturday night and Sunday!

Foolish joy bubbled up inside me and I laughed aloud. Now I could see his presence everywhere. All the warmth and pleasantness the Victorian house lacked were here. I knew I was trespassing when I looked around, but I could not help it. Some deep need made me want to know everything I could about the man who had sent my emotions and desires reeling.

The kitchen showed signs of recent use. A small wood stove had some blackened pots and pans sitting on the round lids. Tooley would have had a fit at their condition, but they were clean and ready for use. I tried to imagine Kipp preparing meals here, but I couldn't. It was a side of him I'd never seen. How little I knew about this stranger who dominated my thoughts and stirred passions that I never dreamed existed.

I stood in the doorway of a small bedroom, looking at the feather bed with its iron bedstead. It was mussed, and I was tempted to smooth the covers and make it up for him. I laughed at myself. I wanted to play house—sweep the floor, cook a meal, and greet Kipp at the door when he came back. And, yes, I wanted to sleep with him in that bed! The thought made me stiffen against an ache that spiraled through hidden, intimate crevices of my body. For a moment I was lost in a fantasy of living here with him. Then I mentally shook myself. What romantic foolishness. I must not intrude upon his privacy. This was his hideaway, his sanctuary. He came here to be alone.

But in the next instant that premise was shattered. As I turned to leave, a crumpled piece of cloth on the floor caught my eye. I picked it up. It was a pale green lady's glove with a slight rip in the thumb. Like the thunderous roar of a tornado, recognition flung a memory back at me. *The mystery lady.* A faint scent of musk rose to my nostrils and I knew with sickening certainty that Kipp had not been here alone after all.

10

I tossed the hateful glove into the fireplace with a sob and then slumped down in the large wing chair, struggling against a wave of anger, hurt, and despair. I tried to reason with myself. There was no reason to feel devastated. All the signs of Kipp's rakish behavior had been there from the moment he pulled me wickledly against him with his cane and poised those compelling lips close to mine. He had mistaken me for Millie's new boarder, and apparently he had not delayed long in meeting the intriguing mystery lady with her veiled face. He must have liked her, for he had brought her here to his private place. The knowledge was bitter. After he had gallantly rescued me from the cliff, he must have come here to dally with a woman who wore pale green and smelled of musk.

I covered my face with my hands and accepted with a sob what my body already knew—I was in love with him! Terribly, horribly, completely in love with him. Just thinking of him with another woman was like a grappling hook tearing at my insides.

I don't know how long I sat there until a rumble of thunder penetrated my consciousness. I jerked up and wiped my tear-streaked face. What was the matter with me? I must leave before a heavy rain caught me and stranded me here. The cabin now seemed horrid and mocking and all my pleasure in it had fled. I couldn't leave fast enough. I wondered if my sixth sense had picked up the woman's presence even before I entered the cabin. Or could she have watched my arrival? I didn't care. There was too much pain in trying to interpret the message my intuition was giving me.

Outside, I ignored the fast-rolling dark clouds and hurried around the side of the cabin. Fancy was snorting and pulling on her reins. Wind whipped her mane. Her eyes rounded as senses were alerted to the coming storm. Overhead, the sun was hidden behind billowing thunderheads massed together in a black mantle. We left the cabin at a near-gallop, heading back through the forested tunnel. Spears of light no longer sliced through the gathering darkness.

Gusts of wind lashed needled branches into a frenzy. Chilled air whipped my hair and bonnet and bit into my face. I was too upset and angry to be afraid. The rush of air chilled my heated face, and my pent-up emotions seemed to find release in the threatening thunder and the assaulting winds. My tears dried on my cheeks and my shattered spirit began to be healed by the force of nature exploding around me.

By the time we reached the main bridle path, I knew that rain was imminent. Chad had warned me that a cloudburst could send dangerous waters rushing down the steep slopes and gullies. I hesitated. I did not want to be navigating a narrow path hugging the mountainside with my horse slipping and sliding on a steep incline. Without weighing my decision, I reined Fancy to the left and we headed downward toward the sloping roof of Lucretia's Poole's house, which was now visible through the trees.

Once more Fancy seemed to know the way. The first large drop of rain hit my face as we reached the modest clapboard house with its white picket fence. Fancy headed toward an open barn at the rear of the house and bounded into the shelter. No one greeted me as I dismounted, so I left her in a stall munching on some hay.

I let myself through a gate and rushed up on a wide veranda circling the house. At the front door I raised a knocker just as a clap of thunder set the whole mountain vibrating. A heavy sheet of pounding rain cut off all chance of darting back to the barn. The storm had hit.

Nervously I waited, then pounded the brass knocker again. Finally, as I was about to despair, I saw the brass doorknob turn.

A frown creased Lucretia's face as she opened the door, and her expression did not soften when she saw who was standing there.

"I . . . I was out riding . . . and got caught by the storm," I said with a rush.

Without smiling or giving me any polite word

of welcome, she motioned me into a narrow entry with two doors opening on each side, one a day parlor, the other a small library. I could see signs that Lucretia had been working over some large ledgers on a crowded desk. There was a crisp efficiency about the house and its furnishings which did not invite unexpected guests in the middle of the day.

"I don't want to bother you," I said as an apology. "If I could just wait out the storm . . ."

Another vibrating roll of thunder echoed my words, and pounding rain fell in torrents upon the roof. "Why would any sensible person go riding with a storm brewing?" she demanded as if I were some errant pupil caught in a culpable act. Her green eyes deliberately traveled over my modest riding habit and my hair, which was blown into untidy tendrils around my face. I resisted the impulse to smooth it.

"It wasn't raining when I started out." I wanted to bite back the words. I didn't want to tell her where I'd been or how long I'd sat in the cabin trying to get control of my emotions. I wondered if my face showed traces of the tears that had eased down my cheeks. "If this is too much of an intrusion—"

"As a matter of fact, I've been wanting to speak with you," she said with a dismissing wave of her hand. "Please come in the parlor. I'll have Mary bring in some tea."

I followed her into a room that was in harmony with the woman's austere, uncluttered appearance. A straight-backed sofa, dark walnut with a sensible tweed covering, sat primly against a wall, with a large picture of the sea, narrowly framed, hanging above it. I wondered if the painting had some special meaning for her. Could it be a scene from her home on the eastern seacoast? That night at dinner, Lucretia had vowed that she wasn't homesick for the sea, but, when I saw the painting, I couldn't help wondering if she told the truth. However, nothing in her manner invited such a personal question, so I said nothing about it as I sat down in an armless chair that forced me to keep my back straight and my knees primly together.

Lucretia struck a match and fed the flame to a hurricane lamp and turned it up to dispel some of the gloom. I wished she would light the waiting paper and wood waiting in a small fireplace, but she didn't. Obviously such pampering would not be permitted in this house. Everything seemed as stoic as the mistress herself.

"Excuse me a moment." She nodded her head curtly. "I'll tell my housekeeper to prepare the tea cart." She left the room, her hidden petticoats swishing under her brown bombazine gown. As always, she carried herself erect, with that no-nonsense, martinet air.

Her absence from the room gave me time to remove my hat and fashion my hair back in a smooth twist. I wondered what she wanted to talk to me about. Did she know about Kipp's amorous tête-à-têtes in the cabin? Was she one of the women he brought there? I couldn't visualize them as lovers—it was even a challenge to visualize Lucretia without her whalebone corset. Who knows, I thought, maybe under all that crispness lay a soft, yielding woman. I lowered my eyes as she came back in the room, fearful that she might read my wayward thoughts.

"Now, then, I must say that I'm surprised that Kipp allowed an inexperienced person to ride one of his horses," she said directly, seating herself in the middle of the sofa.

"I'm not inexperienced. In fact, Miss Purcell said I was one of the best horsewomen at the school." I knew my bragging was childish, but her attitude seemed to bring that out in me. "If it hadn't been for the sudden storm, I would have returned Fancy safely to the stables without intruding upon your hospitality."

"Handling a horse in these treacherous Rocky Mountains is quite different from bridle paths at a riding stable," she said, dismissing my competency. "But then, you seemed to get into difficulty . . . even on foot. I understand you had a harrowing experience on the ridge."

How did she know that? My expression must have showed my surprise and chagrin.

"My housekeeper, Mary, chats with Tooley from time to time," she said pointedly, as if advising me that she knew everything that went on within the walls of Kipp's home.

At least Kipp hadn't told her, I thought, strangely relieved. I could not stand the thought of them discussing me.

"Mary and Tooley are just acquaintances, you understand. I wouldn't let her become involved with that . . . that Irishman!"

"I find Tooley to be a very likable person," I countered.

She sniffed as if to say: You would. At that moment a rose-cheeked woman, plump, wearing a simple cotton dress and apron, pushed a tea cart into the room.

"Mary, this is Miss Allison Lacey."

"Nice to meet you, ma'am." She bobbed her red head. Her wide smile was reflected in her hazel eyes and I liked her immediately. "I'm glad to see you wasn't hurt in your fall the other day."

"I'm fine—"

"Thank you, Mary, that will be all," Lucretia dismissed her officiously. She obviously didn't want to encourage any chitchat between me and her servant.

I thought Mary gave me a half-wink as she turned away, and I had to smother a desire to laugh. Lucretia might think she had this woman under control, but I doubted it very much. The idea of Mary and Tooley courting behind Lucretia's back was a possibility that I thoroughly enjoyed.

The hot, fragrant tea was delightful and I found my spirits rising with every sip. Boldly I let my eyes settle on my hostess. I no longer felt intimidated by her. This feeling of confidence should have been a warning, but I let her lead the conversation as I munched some tiny crescent cookies that had a fresh-baked smell.

She spent the next few minutes lecturing me about the dangers of wild animals, cliffs, and abandoned diggings. "I'm certain that Kipp intended for you to remain in the pasture. He would hate to lose a good horse." Once again her needled remark was an open insult—as if my welfare were of no concern, only the horse's. How abrasive she was! That word described her whole personality as far as I was concerned. How could Kipp stand her?

"And how is Philippe coming along?" she inquired with her nostrils quivering slightly.

It was an open-ended question that had all the signs of a trap. Her inquiry had the same impatient edge to it I had heard when she spoke of him before. "What do you mean?" I countered.

"It's no secret he's quite slow . . . such a shame for Kipp to have a dullard for a son."

"He's not dull at all! In fact, I'm convinced Philippe's a smart little boy. Any lack in learning may be the result of emotional problems."

She scoffed. "Life is never easy for the young, and there's no reason to excuse his lack of achievement. He's seven years old and can't even write his name!"

"He will catch up on his letters and numbers once he—"

"Has someone like you to teach him, I suppose," she finished sarcastically.

"What he needs is someone to take some time with him. He's been shifted from pillar to post and he's terribly insecure."

"He's spoiled, truculent, and in need of a firm hand. I've told Kipp so ever since the boy arrived. He lies and steals and won't have anything to do with anybody but that drunken Tooley!"

147

"I think Tooley's good for him."

"A drunk?" she spat.

"A very warm human being who loves the child. And that seems to be a short commodity in Philippe's life. Given time, I'm certain Kipp will bring him around. His mother must have poisoned the boy's mind against his father, but it's obvious Kipp cares for him very much."

"It's also obvious that Kipp allows himself to be manipulated by everyone. I intend to be quite honest with you," Lucretia said as she launched the first volley in what I soon discovered was a well-planned line of attack. "I cannot sit idly by and watch Kipp being exploited in such a detestable fashion. Getting involved with your aunt has put an albatross around his neck."

My cup made a clicking noise as I set it down.

"Kipp took that horrid hotel off your aunt's hands and has had nothing but bad luck ever since. And now his generous nature is being abused again. It's not enough that he's saddled himself with a senile old woman, but to have her relatives move in on him! He doesn't need this kind of extra worry and expense."

"I have no intention of moving in on anyone. At the moment, we are temporarily his guests, and I fail to see how it is really your business."

"Kipp Halstead is very much my business. He has been ever since he first grubstaked my husband and we survived during those first days when men were fighting, cheating, and killing each other like wild dogs. When we came here, Glen Eyrie was nothing but tents and shacks and filth and ugliness . . . and we've made it into a civilized town. Kipp and I—we've built it! It's our town. And no scheming little twit is going to move in and get her greedy hands on it. You've come too late to lay a claim on Kipp Halstead, Miss Lacey! In this country, jumping claims applies to men as well as gold— and invites the same kind of swift retaliation." The stony green of her eyes was honed to a biting hardness.

Anger made my tone as crisp as hers. "My only concern is my aunt's welfare, and removing her from this place as quickly as possible." I wondered then if she had been the one to shove me over the cliff. Jealousy coated every word she had been saying. I couldn't help but nettle her. "And I'm certain Kipp is able to handle his personal affairs without inviting your interference."

"Unfortunately, Kipp has no judgment about women. Tim and I were always trying to protect him from being taken by some scheming trollop. He has no sense where a pretty face is concerned. Marianne was a good example. He went off to Denver on a business trip, met a storekeeper's daughter who fluttered her eyelashes at him, and he married her. Marianne caused him nothing but grief and pain. She was a scheming bitch of the first order, but nothing was too good for her in his mind."

"He must have loved her—"

"Love," she scoffed. "He never could see beyond her pretty face until she showed her true colors and took off with some rich bounder. Even after Kipp gave her that house and all

149

those wonderful family heirlooms, it wasn't enough for the selfish little piece." She tightened her lips. "I'm not going to sit idly by and see it happen again. I've seen the way you look at him. I know all the signs—"

"No, you're mistaken!" I lied. "I have no plans to trap Kipp Halstead, as you have implied. First of all, I'm ready to leave his house as soon as possible." A remembered musk smell accompanied my words. "I have no interest in Kipp Halstead!"

"Good. How much money do you need?"

The blunt question took me unawares. I echoed, "Money?" Was she offering to pay my travel expenses?

"Don't be coy. I should have said how much money do you *want*? I'm prepared to be generous. Kipp means a great deal to me. Shall we say a thousand dollars? That should return you to Kansas in style."

My fists clenched until the nails bit into the flesh. I couldn't speak. How dare she!

"A thousand dollars—that's more than you can get from Kipp at the moment. He's strapped for funds. One more reversal and he'll go under."

Anger made my tone sharp and accusing. "But you'll be there, of course, to lend a helping hand." I felt ill.

"Yes. Now, how soon can you leave?"

I stood up. "As soon as my aunt is able to travel. But I must refuse your generous offer to buy me off. I don't want Kipp Halstead, but if I did, you wouldn't have enough money in your clutching hands to pry me away."

Her eyes narrowed. "I see. Well, there are other means of persuasion."

"Is that a threat?"

"Of course not, dear. Just a friendly warning . . . between friends." Her narrow teeth showed in a smile. "Would you like some more tea?"

"No, thank you. The storm has passed . . . and I feel the need for a clean breath of fresh air!"

I didn't wait for her to see me out.

11

I had to get my wayward feelings about Kipp under control before they brought me to the brink of disaster. He was always in my thoughts, even though I avoided him as much as possible the next week—which wasn't difficult, since he left early and came home late, usually after I was in bed. He seemed to be pushing himself as hard as he could to get the smelter in operation, and I wondered about the seriousness of his financial situation. Lucretia blamed his reverses on bad luck, but I wondered. Since I didn't like the woman, it was easy for me to suspect her of trying to ruin Kipp so he would have to accept her financial help—with strings attached, of course. I prayed he would be able to stay out of her clutches. I hesitated to ask him about my aunt's financial affairs. Any questions might imply that I thought him guilty of stealing her money as well as her hotel. There must be another way to discover whether or not she had any funds that would see us safely away from Glen Eyrie. I had no idea how to cope with her illness with what little funds I had left from my summer salary.

I spent every morning with Aunt Esther. Her walking improved and I often took her down the hall to sit in my room for a change of scenery. Every day I hoped for some sign that she was coming out of her deep trauma, but she remained passive, detached, and when she spoke, it was out of context with reality. However, sometimes her brow would crease as if she were trying to draw something out from the murky depths of her mind.

"What is it, Aunt Esther?" I prodded. If only she would speak to me, tell me what had happened to cause the vicious blow to her head. I sensed that something vital to her welfare was locked in the shadows of her mind.

She would look at me as if about to answer my question, and my heart would lurch wildly. Then her brow would smooth as if the nagging thread had been snapped. She'd turn vacant eyes on me and say something like, "Time to bring the cows in." Tears would spill into my eyes and I had to turn away quickly. Even though her physical condition had improved, there was little sign that her mind was healing.

Winning Philippe's friendship was another challenge. Our daily contact proved to be frustrating, with a lack of any real progress. He tolerated my presence only because his father had ordered him to do as I said. I decided not to challenge him about my fall, since such questioning might only build the wall higher. Tooley said someone had tried to turn him against me.

It seemed exactly like something Lucretia would do, and the thought made me more determined than ever to win Philippe over.

I went into the library, as Kipp had suggested, to look for some books that I might use with Philippe. Once again, I was delighted by the shelves and shelves of leather-bound volumes, and it was difficult for me to remember my purpose as my eyes feasted on numerous titles I would enjoy reading. Kipp was certainly eclectic in his tastes, I mused, if his library was any indication that he had read widely in all the subjects. What a delight it would be to discuss some of the topics with him. Then I chided myself for indulging in such fantasy, and I renewed my effort to find some suitable volumes for capturing Philippe's interest.

Finally, on the bottom shelf of a glassed-in bookcase I found several children's readers. I wondered if they could have been Kipp's, for they looked well worn. I was about to close the case when my eyes caught a glimpse of a photograph folder. I opened it and found myself staring at a brown tintype of Kipp and a pretty young woman in a wedding gown. Marianne! My eyes fastened greedily on her face. Fair hair fell in long curls around a petite face. Her eyes were oval and accented a slender, tilted nose. A slight, coquettish smile hovered on a mouth curved with the shape of a cupid's bow. I despaired to see how lovely his bride had been. Kipp looked years younger, and I realized how his smooth face had recorded the trials and battles that he'd fought since this picture had been taken. I shut the folder and put it back on the shelf.

Once more I had intruded into his personal life—and once more I had been hurt.

I took myself in hand and tried to write a letter to Emmett. With my quill pen poised above the paper, I realized that I couldn't remember what he looked like. His features were vague, as if the tide of time had already blurred them. Even the "Dear Emmett" looked strange and slightly ridiculous. I bit the end of my pen. The only subject I really wanted to talk about was Kipp Halstead. How could I describe the scenery without mentioning the man who dominated it? How could I tell about Aunt Esther without mentioning the part Kipp played in the drama, and the worrisome suspicions that would not go away? How could I even write about Philippe without mentioning his father or the coquettish blond mother whose picture I had just seen? I couldn't. I tore up the paper and vowed to try another day. I penned a quick note to Miss Purcell which stated simply that I had arrived safely. It seemed as if I was suspended between two worlds and belonged in neither.

That afternoon I asked Philippe if he would like to make some name cards for the rock specimens. I knew that classification was a good technique for teaching sight words, and for diagnosing how well he could print his letters. He suspiciously agreed and I almost got a slight smile out of him as I settled him at his father's desk in the library. I had raised the seat with a large dictionary and he seemed almost awed by his position at the desk. I didn't know what his father would say, but I didn't care. This was the only room that didn't hold the cold dank air of the rest of the house. I gave him pen and paper with a list of words to copy on cards.

He labored over each letter and I smothered a smile when I saw his tongue caught at the corner of his mouth as he worked. We did only a couple each day, but he seemed less brittle as we put the smudged cards in the case to identify quartz, crystals, and agates. I noticed that the amethyst stone was still gone, but I wasn't going to jeopardize the improvement in our relationship with any suspicious questioning.

Every afternoon we worked in the library, and when he was tired of printing, I started reading James Fenimore Cooper's *The Last of the Mohicans* to him. Even though he was still keeping his guard up and scowling at me with those dagger eyes, I was encouraged. He was a bright little boy and if given half a chance, he might come around. A lot would depend how he made out at school in the fall. This reminded me that my interest in him could be only temporary, and I wondered if he would feel betrayed again when I left.

I used Fancy as an excuse to talk with Ching Lee. Sometimes I took the mare for a short gallop around the small pasture or just stroked her neck while she dipped her head over the stall gate. Ching was always hovering near, and I complimented him on Fancy's shiny coat and the soft leather saddle and harnesses, which showed signs of ardent oiling.

"You are very good with horses. Did my aunt and uncle have horses for you to care for?"

"No. I work in livery stable down the street part-time. I not good in hotel . . . with people. Meestah Ben let me get different job."

"Then you weren't at the hotel when he had his accident."

His eyes narrowed to slits. "He not fall I been there."

"What do you mean?"

"I take care Meestah Ben. He good man. I not let him fall."

"You think that somebody . . . let him fall?" I pried.

"I no say. I not work at hotel that day, I gone to livery stable."

"Who was with him that day?"

"No say. He busy changing kitchen . . . putting in new things, building racks for wine cellar. Then he fall. I no see what happen. Not my fault."

"Of course not. I wasn't blaming you." It seemed to me I had said the same thing to SuLang about Aunt Esther's "accident." These two people who loved my aunt and uncle were terribly defensive, as if harboring guilt. Maybe it was nothing more than the usual "if I had only" scenario that all of us go through when we use hindsight. In any case, I had learned nothing from Ching Lee that I didn't already know. And yet I felt a clue was still there if I could just find it.

On Thursday afternoon Kipp arrived home

earlier and found Philippe and me still sitting in the library reading.

"School dismissed," Kipp said airily. "I've come to take your teacher horseback riding." He ruffled Philippe's hair and I was gratified to see that the boy didn't pull away. "Scoot and tell Tooley I'll be home for dinner tonight." As Philippe bounded out of the room, Kipp grinned at me. "The last piece of machinery has been installed in the smelter. Go change and we'll take a ride."

I hesitated. As always, his presence swept away my well-ordered existence and sent it into chaos. I had a little speech all prepared in case he asked me to go riding, informing him that I preferred to do my riding alone, but in the face of his exuberance, the words faded away and I could only stammer, "Thank you, but—"

"Come on!" He brushed aside the rest of my refusal. Laughing, he took the book from my hand and pulled me to my feet. "Go change, I want to show it to you." He looked younger, more like the photograph, the planes of his face smooth and his facial muscles relaxed. I knew then how much pressure he'd been under. At the moment it did not seem to matter that I knew he kept company with someone else. He was here, smiling at me, wanting to include me in his life. That was enough. I would sort out my ambivalent feelings later. I rushed upstairs and changed into my riding habit.

I wondered if Lucretia saw us go by as we rode down the bridle path past her house. For a moment I entertained a sense of foreboding, but it quickly faded as Kipp laughed and chatted beside me on Midnight. A spicy pine scent filled the air, and gay splashes of color from the wild irises growing near the creek's edge gave the day a mood of spring and youth. We followed Timber Creek until we reached the railroad tracks. We kicked our horses into a gallop, and a short distance beyond, we came to a huge wooden building bearing a new sign, "Halstead Smelter Company."

Kipp put his hands on my waist and lightly swung me down from the saddle. For a moment his touch lingered there, and it took all my willpower to remain rigid and not lean into him. Laughing as if he knew full well how his embrace affected me, he slipped his arm around my waist and drew me to the door.

Inside the building the odor of clean sawdust greeted my nostrils with the freshness of newly cut timbers. A vaulted ceiling was crisscrossed with huge beams holding up giant wheels, mammoth chutes, and iron plungers large enough to crush a man's head. Everything had been oiled and polished, and numerous machines waited like disjointed iron creatures ready to start rumbling.

Eagerly Kipp described the techniques of processing raw ore as he showed me around. He bragged that he had fashioned his smelter after one built by Professor Nathaniel Hill of Brown University which employed the latest milling methods known. "No need to ship raw ore out of the area now," he said proudly. "I've sunk my last dollar into this smelter. Glen Eyrie will become the shipping center for mines all over this area. It's a dream come true." His deep laughter echoed to the high rafters. He grabbed me in a wild spin as his exuberance spilled over and he twirled me across the floor.

I was still gasping for breath when he pulled me up a flight of stairs to his new office. "I'll be moving out of the hotel now and bringing all my things here. Well, what do you think?"

His office was a large room under the eaves, with natural wood giving the walls a polished, golden look. "I'm very impressed."

He pulled me over to a window at one end and we looked out upon a panorama of high peaks and red cliffs. My head reeled from the majestic beauty—and his nearness. His arm tightened around my waist. "It's God's country, Allie. It gets in your blood and won't let you go."

"Yes," I murmured, knowing even as I said it that I too had succumbed to this wild country and that something deep inside, untouched before, leapt to embrace it.

"Allie . . ." He turned, his eyes fixed on me now and his warm breath bathing my face. I knew if I raised my face to his he would kiss me—and I would be lost. The knowledge that he gave those lips freely brought too much pain. I backed away quickly.

"What's the matter?" he asked, perplexed as I walked away.

"Nothing . . . but I think we'd better go." All the joy of lighthearted companionship was gone. I started down the steps without waiting for him. In my haste I caught the hem of my riding skirt, and would have fallen if he had not reached out and caught me.

"No," I said hoarsely. The stair railing was at my back as he pressed against me. His lips took mine. Remembered desire sprang unbidden at his touch. Even as I fought to deny the wave of pleasure spiraling through me, my arms went around his neck. I felt warm and safe and fully alive in his embrace. I returned his kisses. There was no escape from the bittersweet truth that I loved him.

He trailed his lips across my cheek and buried his face in the soft, pulsating crevice of my neck. "You are an enchantress, Allie," he murmured, "with those topaz eyes and beguiling lips. And your chin . . . " He lightly cupped it and kissed the tip of it. "Do you know how devastating it is when you're angry? Jutting out, taunting me with that proper, schoolmarm manner . . . daring me to touch, caress, and kiss away that outward crispness . . . and delight in the wild, untamed desire that's hiding there."

His mouth caught mine again and I felt his tongue tasting the sweetness of my parted lips. I was lost in rising spirals of a building need that made me lean into his virile body even as I faintly gasped, "Let me go . . . please."

His hands molded my soft swelling breasts and he groaned as my heightened breathing mingled with his. Then abruptly he moved back, apparently as shaken as I. "What you do to a man should be against the law, Allie," he said in a passion-laced voice. "Beware, my love, or I will have my way with you. Even a gentleman would find himself sorely taxed trying to keep his distance—and I'm no gentleman." He said it lightly, with a quirking of his lips, but its truth bit into me with savage pain.

"Yes, I know." His confession had brought me back to reality with an abruptness that labeled me the lovesick fool that I was.

We said little on the ride back, and I wondered if he could possibly be aware of the terrible conflict going on within me. I loved this man, and despite all signs that he was nothing more then a devilish rogue who took what pleased him at the moment, I could not turn back from a path of destruction. I had no romantic experiences to draw upon.

When we returned to the house, I should have excused myself from dinner, but my need to be with him outweighed my pride or good judgment. He opened a bottle of champagne for a celebration, and his high spirits were infectious.

It was understandable that I should become a willing victim of his charm. There had been too much loneliness in my life, too many bland meals in the company of dull faculty members who talked about the same things term after term. The names of the students changed, but that was all; table conversation at the school was predictable and deadening. I had begun to feel as dull and as boring as Miss Emma Martin, who had been teaching for forty years. Kipp brought back my youth, and I knew that whatever the cost, I must grab at this moment of feeling alive.

We enjoyed Tooley's delicious roast beef and the succulent, tender vegetables he had cooked in one of his special sauces. Kipp instilled every subject with an effervescence that matched our bubbling champagne. I put aside all my doubts. I found myself laughing and making witty remarks that astounded even me. I would offer a turn of phrase . . . he'd cap it . . . I'd add a twist or pun that would send us off into laughter.

I knew that nothing was really that funny, but I was riding on a crest of euphoria. The more I tried to pull myself together and act primly, the easier it seemed to abandon myself to being happy. I forgot to be wary of his charm. His soft eyes caressed my face and my will weakened.

We chatted and teased each other, and when our hands touched, a searing warmth invaded the spot. Every lazy smile he gave me heightened my awareness. The lamplight seemed to flicker brighter and my senses tingled with a rush of stimuli. Time had no meaning for me— and then the wonderful bubble broke.

In the middle of an entertaining story about a play he'd seen in the Winter Garden Theater in New York City, he suddenly broke off. His stunned expression brought my head around with a jerk.

Aunt Esther!

Standing in the doorway, she was a frail, haunted specter, her blue eyes wide and frantic. She waved her hands wildly as she screamed at me, "It's the hotel, Allison. Run, child, run!"

The moment froze like the frame of a nightmare. Then both Kipp and I leapt from our chairs and sped to her side.

"What is it? What about the hotel?" Kipp prodded.

Aunt Esther looked up into his face, gave a shrill whimper, and then crumpled.

Kipp swung her up in his arms and carried her to her bedroom, where SuLang had just arrived with a dinner tray. She nearly dropped it when Kipp rushed in and laid Aunt Esther on the bed. By this time my aunt was issuing high-pitched wails that tore at the heart. SuLang lashed out at me. "What did you do to her?"

"That's enough, SuLang," Kipp rebuked her. "Esther came downstairs on her own."

"I . . . I didn't know she could navigate the stairs," I stammered. Had she sought me out in a lucid moment? What had she been trying to tell me? *It's the hotel!* What did the warning mean? And whom was she warning me against? Involuntarily my eyes fixed on Kipp's handsome face. I dared not ask him what he thought she had meant. If he were responsible for the events that had closed down the hotel, he would only lie to me. And if he were innocent, he would be angry at such questions.

"There, she's settled down now," said Kipp as he took my arm. "SuLang will see to her."

The plunge down from the soaring romantic heights had been too much for me. I felt ill.

"You must excuse me."

"Allie—"

I jerked away and did not look at him again as I fled to my room. I shut the door and leaned against it, and stayed there until I heard him go downstairs again. The house grew quiet and I wondered if he had gone to his cabin for the night. Tears flowed down my cheeks. Kipp . . . Kipp. I could not forget the look on my aunt's face as she looked up at him.

It was nearly dawn before I fell into a fitful sleep. I had wrestled with the jagged edges of the diabolical puzzle, but none of the pieces had fallen into place. And deep in the knowing part of my being, I knew that time was running out.

12

I had forgotten about the barn dance on Saturday night until Chad rode by the house and reminded me. I tried to decline but he would not let me go back on my promise.

"Everyone will be there. It's a benefit for the volunteer fire brigade. Young and old and all ages in between will do-si-do to the wildest fiddle playing you've ever heard. It'll do you good to get out and meet folks, Allison. Besides, I want to show up with the prettiest gal on my arm." His freckled face wore a big grin. "Show all them fellows a thing or two. Everybody will be bringing a mound of food and jugs of cider. We'll have a good time." Then he frowned. "You didn't promise to go with Halstead, did you? . . . Good. I didn't think so. He and Lucretia Poole usually take in these affairs together."

I put a bright smile on my face and said that I would love to go.

Saturday morning, Tooley was busy getting cakes and pies ready for the affair. I had learned that he was taking Mary. He asked me if I was going with Kipp to the dance.

I said, "No, he hasn't asked me . . . but I'm going with Jim Chadwick."

Tooley frowned. "With everything on Kipp's mind, I'm a-thinkin' he's forgotten to ask you."

"I understand that he usually escorts Lucretia," I said evenly, downing a rising disappointment. Maybe I shouldn't have accepted Chad. Then feminine pride made me glad that I didn't have to wait around wondering if he were going to take Lucretia or me.

I hadn't seen Kipp for several days. He had been gone from Glen Eyrie most of the week, riding to all the mines in the area, arranging for shipments of ore to his new smelter, and the house became more oppressive than ever in his absence. Aunt Esther began to roam all over the house, eyes glazed, mumbling incoherently. She seemed to be searching for someone or something.

When Dr. Yates came to see her, he shook his head. "She's slipping away from us."

"But she seems stronger."

"Physically, yes. But she shows little sign of being in touch with reality anymore, not even the past. I've seen it happen before. She's in a world of her own now, where we can't reach her. She may prove to be dangerous to herself . . . and others."

"No, I won't believe that! I won't give up!"

I refused to accept her condition as permanent or dangerous. I was glad to see that she was getting physically stronger. I filled my days looking after her in spite of SuLang's silent objections. It was obvious she was jealous of my attachment to Aunt Esther and resented it. She did not understand that I too had shared in Aunt Esther's kindness when I was growing up.

My tutoring lessons with Philippe were a challenge. They left me emotionally drained. Some days he was only high-spirited, but others he was a belligerent little devil.

One afternoon he was particularly trying. "I won't do it—I won't!" He flung all the letter patterns on the floor and even upset the inkwell. I had to scramble to keep the india ink from ruining everything on Kipp's desk.

That night I went to bed exhausted. I must have been sleeping deeply, but suddenly in the middle of the night my eyes flew wide open. I stiffened. My senses quivered. My room was alive with shadows—and one of them moved! A figure loomed closer to my bed.

My heartbeat stopped.

I jerked to one side just as a pillow came down on my face. Gasping for air, I shoved it away. Then I cried with horror as I stumbled to my feet. For a moment I couldn't see who it was. Then I cried, "Aunt Esther! Aunt Esther! It's me, Allison."

My words did not penetrate her trance. Her face was without recognition. I knew it was not her beloved niece she had just tried to smother, but someone else. She had completely lost touch with reality, just as Dr. Yates had warned. But who was it she thought she had under that pillow? Some twisted desire for revenge drove her, but against whom? The answer was locked up in her crazed mind. For the first time, I was positive that my aunt knew who had struck her.

As I led her back to her bed, I could not help but wonder with a shudder if she had intended to find Kipp's bedroom across the landing from mine.

I lay awake the rest of that night and arose with dark shadows ringing my eyes. By the time daylight rimmed the edges of my windows, I had reached a decision. As soon as Kipp returned, I would tell him.

Kipp came back the day of the dance, and I told him what had happened. "My God, she's gone mad! We'll have to put someone with her day and night . . . and keep the doors locked. I won't take a chance on something like that happening again."

"SuLang handles her better than anyone else."

"Then I'll hire a girl to relieve her of her other duties."

"I'd be glad to help, but . . ." I steeled myself to tell him of the decision I had made to leave Glen Eyrie. Before I could, he delayed my remarks by asking, "How is Philippe coming along?"

"I'm pleased. He has a quick mind, and can learn when he wants to apply himself."

"You're wonderful with him, Allie. He's changing . . . and it's all due to you." His face softened and I had to look away from it to maintain any kind of professional manner.

"No, I told you it would just take time . . . and love. It would be advisable for you to find someone to continue the tutoring when I leave—"

"Leave?"

"I have decided that I am of no help to my aunt. SuLang is right. I only add to her distress. From the first, Esther did not want me to remain here, and I . . . I have decided that it is best that I obey her wishes. Until I am able to make different arrangements for her, we are grateful for your hospitality, but Lucretia is right: you should not be obligated for her keep—or mine."

"Damn Lucretia," he swore. Black anger tightened the muscles in his face. "What has been going on since I've been gone? Has Lucretia been here trying to take charge?"

"No. I have come to my own decision, without any regard for her opinion." Or her money, I added silently. My life would be more desolate at the school than ever before, and this knowledge saddened and depressed me so much that I could not look at him.

"It sounds to me as if you're running away." He flung the words as a challenge, but I didn't rise to the bait. He knew better than anyone else how impossible the present situation was.

"There is nothing to keep me here," I lied, keeping my gaze fixed somewhere below that square chin. "And I'm not leaving because I'm afraid for my own safety—"

"But of your own feelings, perhaps," he taunted.

My anger flared and words choked in my throat. How could he flaunt my feelings in my face this way? I was not one of his fancy women sharing kisses and caresses as an idle sport. I wanted to lash out and tell him I knew all about his love nest in the woods. Even now I wondered if he had been away on business as he said, or if he'd been dallying in his cabin with feminine company. "I've thought it over and I must leave."

"I'm sorry, Allie," he said gently. "I didn't mean to react like that. You took me by surprise. Let's take time to talk this over. I hurried back today so we could go to the firemen's barn dance tonight. We'll have a good time and put everything else out of our minds for one night."

"But you . . . you didn't say anything about the dance," I stammered.

"Sorry, too many things on my mind, I guess, but it's a big community affair, for our volunteer fire brigade—"

"Yes, I know."

"And it will be a kind of celebration too—launching my new business. Put on your best bib and tucker and we'll have ourselves a grand time." A boyish enthusiasm lit up his eyes.

I swallowed. "Kipp, I didn't know you were planning on taking me tonight, and . . . and I already have an escort. Chad asked me a couple of weeks ago, when we went to church. If only you had said something."

I sensed controlled fury as he said crisply, "Yes, yes, I see now that I have been presumptuous." His smile was cold and thin. "I just assumed that you would want to go with me. I apologize." He gave me a mock bow.

"Kipp, please, I—"

"Don't distress yourself. I'm certain you will enjoy it."

"Will . . . will I see you there?" I feared that he wouldn't go now that I had refused him. He needed to relax, enjoy himself, and forget about the exhausting grind of getting his smelter in operation. I was relieved when he said, "Of course, my dear. You must save me a dance."

"Yes, yes, I will," I promised, knowing such intimacy would only make my decision to leave harder.

He seemed satisfied. "Good. Now I must see what scrumptious dishes Tooley has prepared for the event. He will bring them down later with Philippe. It will do us all good to have a gala time tonight, won't it?" There was a smile on his lips but no warmth in his eyes as he left me.

I chose to wear a simple yellow summer dress I'd had for several seasons. The lace edging was still firm and the full skirt and saucy peplum would be good for dancing, I decided. It would go well with my one pair of soft beige slippers. Fashioned of checkered dimity with a modest neckline and butterfly sleeves, the dress would be comfortably cool for the vigorous exercise square dancing demanded. I pulled my hair back tightly with a green velvet ribbon to hold it off my neck, and I let the streamers trail over the dangling curls. Then I flung a white knit shawl over my shoulders to guard against the evening's coolness.

From the moment Chad and I arrived at the spacious barn with its bright lanterns and toe-tapping music, I could not keep my eyes from searching the crowd for Kipp. He had left earlier in the buggy, and my heart wrenched when I thought I could have been sitting there beside him. I wondered if he were bringing Lucretia or one of his other ladies.

Like the barn dances back home, there were people of all ages in new, old, fancy, and plain attire. On the dance floor, faded gingham dresses and homespun cotton shirts blended with doe-skin trousers and fringed jackets.

For the first time, I felt perfectly at ease with the inhabitants of Glen Eyrie and exchanged smiles and greetings with them as Chad and I pushed through the laughing crowd. Youngsters darted around the edges of the floor in games of their own, just missing stomping boots and flying slippers as dancers followed instructions from a tall, lanky fellow with an Adam's apple quivering in his throat as he called out in bass tones, "Alamand left . . . with a grand right and left . . . meet your partner and promenade home . . ."

Three fiddle players, one short with a handlebar mustache almost as big as he was, and two looking like cowboys with bandy legs, sawed away at the lively tunes. Before I knew it, I was out on the floor with my yellow skirts whirling and my ribbon streamers flying as Chad swung me around.

I lost track of the time. Before I could catch my breath from one dance, I was back on the floor with Chad as we joined hands in a round dance or another square. I decided Kipp had lied to me about coming. He had left the house before I did, so he should have been here by now, unless . . . I bit my lip as I finished the thought. Unless he had found something or someone more interesting elsewhere.

I tried to put him out of my mind. I needed a release from depression and conflicting emotions. During the last few days my nerves had become frayed. The problems with Philippe and the hopeless condition of my aunt made my days and nights tense and depressing. My decision to leave had been the final twist. I needed to give myself up to lively music and the joy of dancing. I laughed with Chad and allowed myself to blush as he proudly claimed me dance after dance.

I don't know how long Kipp had been standing near the door before I saw him. The way he was staring at the dancers, I had the feeling I had made a fool of myself in front of him. Had he been watching my giddy behavior? Would he come and claim his dance with me . . . or did that glower mean that he was going to ignore the request he had made for a dance?

"I'm tired. Can we sit this one out?" I said to Chad, jerking my gaze away from the handsome figure in blue frock coat and tight trousers. If Kipp wanted his dance, he would have to come after it. I would not let him know how my heart was racing at the thought of twirling around the room in his arms.

"Let me get you another cup of cider," Chad

said when he had escorted me to a bale of hay which served nicely as a seat between dances.

"Yes, that would be nice."

He pushed through the crowd, and once more my eyes sought the place where I had seen Kipp standing. It was empty. Where had he gone? I stood up and let my eyes boldly circle the room.

"Looking for someone?" He was at my elbow with that infuriating grin on his face.

I started to lie and then laughed instead. "Yes . . . you."

"That's what I thought. Come on, let's get out of here."

"Didn't you come to claim your dance?"

"Yes, but I'd rather do my dancing alone . . . to more mellow music." He winked roguishly and cupped my elbow, pulling me toward an open side door.

"But I can't leave."

"Of course, you can."

"Chad . . ." I looked back.

"Chad be damned. He's had you for nearly two hours—it's my turn." He gave me that maddening smile which left little resistance against his charm.

I knew that I was behaving improperly. A lady did not leave her escort and go off into the night with someone else. I was horrified at myself for doing it, but I went with him without further protest.

"This way." In another moment we were outside. I had forgotten my shawl, but the crisp breeze felt good against my flushed face. It was a beautiful night, a spangled sky all purple and silver with a round, silken moon moving majestically across it.

"Where are we going?"

"Down to the creek."

"But—"

"You promised me a dance, and I'm going to claim it." His playful mood was infectious and I giggled foolishly as he put his arm around my waist and we walked across a small clearing. I breathed in deeply and let myself thrill to the moment. His vigorous profile caught the moonlight and once again I was aware of the rugged strength registered there.

The floating strains of music became fainter as he led me away from the barn, through a thin band of lodgepole pines. A lovers' moon spread a gentle wash of silver light upon the ground as we reached a grassy area made by the curve of a miniature creek.

"Here we are—our own private dance floor." He put his arms around me in dance position. His eyes were shining. "Now, isn't this better?" He began to hum a Strauss waltz as he guided me over the patch of smooth grassy ground.

"You're crazy," I laughed in protest as our feet moved in three-quarter time, and we whirled and spun like sprites dancing under the moon. With my head back, I gazed up at him, filled with a happiness I had never known.

"You promised me a dance. Nothing was said about where." He laid his face against my cheek and we moved in rhythm to his deep voice. I forgot about everything but the ecstasy of being in his arms. I knew I would have to store up this memory and hold it firm when time tried to erase it from me. I was very, very happy . . . so happy, I was suddenly crying.

"What . . . what is it?" He stopped dancing. "Did I step cruelly on your feet?"

I shook my head, bewildered by my own emotions.

"Then what?"

"I . . . I don't know."

"I do. You're trying to go against those wonderful instincts of yours. Why don't you just give in to them and quit fighting them, my love."

Beware, my love. I will have my way with you.

Sanity returned and I stiffened in his embrace. "Please . . . we must go back."

"Allie, darling!"

"Stop it!" I couldn't take any more. The beautiful night, dancing under the stars, feeling his arms around me, and under it all, the torture of knowing it meant very little to him. I had tried to pretend that his other women didn't matter, that I would be leaving soon, grateful for a few warm memories to take with me, but his endearments were like salt upon a festering sore. My voice was choked with anger as I lashed out at him. "I'm not one of your paramours—and I know all about them. I found your sweet little love nest in the woods. Oh, yes, I've been to your cabin." Now that I had started, all my anguish poured out like floodwaters. "I know what goes on there." My voice rose hysterically.

He looked as if I'd struck him. "What on earth are you talking about?"

"Your cabin. I rode there one day." I couldn't hold any of it back. "That's where you'd been for a day and a half. And I found her glove there, right by the bedroom door. The bed was still tumbled . . . and . . . and . . ." I buried my hands in my face and sobbed.

He took my hands and eased them down. "Listen to me." His voice was gentle, and moonlight caught like prisms in his eyes. "Yes, I was there. I go to the cabin often to get away from bad memories. But I have never taken a woman there."

"You lie! I found her glove."

"Whose glove? What in God's name are you talking about?"

"The mystery lady—the woman who came up on the train with me, Millie's new boarder. She wore a green glove with a rip on the thumb, and I found it there in your cabin."

His expression should have been laughable, but in my pain I could not see any humor in his utter bewilderment. "But I don't know any mystery lady with a green glove. If she was there, it was without my knowledge."

I wanted to believe him. Lord, how I wanted to believe him. But I couldn't let it go. "Why would she go there if you weren't there?"

"I don't know. I didn't see anyone. Honest, Allie, I slept and read."

"I saw your book." Then my eyes widened. "The bookmark had been moved nearly to the end," I said aloud.

"That proves it, then," he said with a sigh of relief. "As innocent as you are, you must know that I wouldn't get much reading done while engaging in a clandestine affair." He chuckled as he lifted my chin and chided softly, "You have my word."

"As a gentleman?" I managed to tease as I sniffed back my tears.

"No. As someone who loves you very much."

His arms slid around me and I melted against him as if every pore in my body had been waiting for this surrender. I had been wrong about him! There was no need to hold back. His kiss found instant response as I trembled in his embrace. He murmured endearments as his mouth pulled against mine. "How could you have thought I wanted anyone but you? When you told me this morning that you were leaving, that you had no reason for staying, I knew I could not hold back any longer. I wanted to wait until I was sure I wasn't going to be a penniless beggar before saying anything. Even now I have nothing to offer. But you can't leave. I'll be back on my feet financially soon . . ."

I caressed his face and let my hands pull his face to mine. I hardly knew what he was saying. He loved me—that's all that mattered. He hadn't been with another woman! Everything else could be sorted out later.

Our mounting passion threatened to spill beyond our control. "We must go," I murmured huskily.

"Must we?"

"What if Chad comes looking for us?"

"Let him come." His voice was soft and endearing.

"I . . . I have to tell him I'm not going home with him."

"Does that mean you're going home with me?" The question had overtones. The distance across the hall was not much of a barrier in my present state of mind. I think he knew what my answer was when he kissed me again.

Reluctantly we made our way back to the dance. I didn't know how long we had been gone, but long tables had been set outside and food had begun to arrive. I saw Tooley and Philippe right away, and Kipp went to get another basket from the buggy. I was helping Philippe set out plates on one of the tables when Chad appeared at my elbow with Lucretia.

"Hey, where have you been?" he asked, puzzled but in good humor.

Before I could answer, Lucretia said in an accusing voice, "I saw you and Kipp leave by a side door."

"Yes," I answered without any elaboration, smiling sweetly at her. I didn't care that my face was flushed and my lips soft from the warmth of his kisses. I knew I should apologize to Chad for ducking out on him, but how could I when the world was spinning about in a wonderful fashion that made me want to laugh and sing all at the same time?

"Well, where's Kipp now?" Lucretia demanded as if I were guilty of spiriting him away somewhere.

Before I could answer, Kipp returned with

another basket of food, which he handed to Tooley with a groan. "You brought enough for Freeman's army," he teased.

"Set our basket over there, Mary," Lucretia ordered as if she weren't going to be outdone by any offerings from Tooley. I saw Tooley and Mary exchange amused grins. Competition wasn't a part of their relationship.

Philippe reached in and grabbed a chicken leg. I was so delighted to see him happily eating that I refrained from any reprimand, but Lucretia lifted her eyes in a disgusted grimace. She probably would have ordered him away from the table without any supper for such impolite behavior.

The music stopped and there was a rush of people into the yard, all grabbing plates and lining up for the smorgasbord of potluck dishes. The delicious smells of baked beans, fried chicken, and roasted mutton mingled with those of salads, home-grown vegetables, and prize-winning desserts. Tooley was not alone in setting out his offerings with an air of pride. There were others who fancied themselves just as good cooks, and they watched people choose their offerings with an air of parental pride.

"Come on, let's eat." Chad grabbed my arm.

I sent a helpless look at Kipp, but he only winked wickedly. A kind of communication existed between us that shut out all others. We played a lovers' game, pretending not to notice each other, when the air was really charged with a vibrating awareness between us.

Lucretia tried to maneuver Kipp away, but he

stood in the line with Tooley, Mary, and Philippe while Chad and I led the way. Lucretia trailed in the rear, looking like a war frigate about to fire away at me with a vengeance.

Someone poured a glass of cider for me and I set it by my plate as we sat down to eat. I had taken only two sips when Philippe lurched forward to grab a roll off the table and knocked my elbow. I dropped the cup, spilling the rest of it on my gown.

I leapt to my feet and then the ground swirled out from under me. I could not control my breathing. Panic-stricken, I saw Kipp's face through a distorted, thickening wave. A gray mass of nothingness rose to blot out my vision. I fought against the quagmire that pulled me down, down, down . . . until it finally swept me away in an impenetrable sleep.

13

I learned later that my cider had been laced with a fatal dose of laudanum. Philippe had accidentally spilled most of the drink—and saved my life. I slept for nearly two days from the few sips I had taken, and when I fought my way out of the murky depths of drugged sleep, I found Kipp at my bedside.

Unshaven, with a gray pallor on his face, he saw my eyelids flicker upward and said hoarsely, "So you decided to wake up." His teasing was betrayed by a quiver of his lips, and there was a suspicious fullness in his eyes.

"What . . . what happened?" My memory was disjointed and overgrown with half-images. Was I caught in the middle of a dream even now?

He held my hands tightly and avoided answering me directly. "Doc Yates says you're going to be fine. We need to get some food into you. Tooley's been bringing up trays every hour, hoping you would be ready to drink or eat."

My tongue was thick and my mouth parched.

"Water," I managed. The room was still wavering and the bed had a rolling action that made me want to hold on to the sides.

He lifted my head and gently eased the liquid down my throat. Then he cushioned me back against his firm chest, stroking my damp, tousled hair. His lips touched soft kisses along my hairline as he put his head against mine. I tried to stay awake, but my heavy eyelids would not stay open. Waves of drugged sleep came and went. The next time I opened my eyes, he was sitting in the chair again.

He stood up and smiled at me. "Hello again. You look brighter this time, darling. Do you think you could stay awake for a few minutes? I'll get some coffee. We tried some before, but you threw it up in a very unladylike fashion. No, don't look embarrassed—Doc said you got rid of some of the laudanum. But he did say to try coffee again. We'll start with that and see if we can't get rid of some of that limpness." He kissed my forehead. "You look like a marionette doll with the strings cut."

"Who . . . who cut them?" The question came out involuntarily.

His fists clenched and an ugly twist came to his mouth. "God help them if I ever find out!"

It was several days before I really pieced together what had happened, and even then there were too many unanswered questions. I didn't know who had handed me the drugged cider, or if it had been set by my plate. I couldn't remember—too much confusion with people balancing plates, moving about. It was impossible to go back and focus on any one person. Anyone at our table could have done it, or someone else brushing by unnoticed. One fact was stark and clear, however: the act had been deliberate and skillfully executed. If Philippe hadn't upset my drink, I would have been fatally drugged.

Everyone fussed over me—Kipp, Tooley, Chad, and even Philippe, who sidled into my room with a pretty speckled pink stone which he thrust into my hand. The unexpected gift overwhelmed me.

"Don't you like it? I had to wade out in the middle of the creek to get it!" he said in his usual prickly, defensive tone.

"Oh, I love it," I said, blinking rapidly. "It's the prettiest stone I've ever seen. I'll keep it on my dressing table always."

"Are you going to be sick a long time?"

I laughed. " 'Fraid not. It's back to lessons in a day or two."

"Oh." I could not tell from his expression whether he was disappointed or pleased, but at least his habitual scowl was gone, and I took that as a good sign. I wondered if he knew he had saved my life by upsetting my drink. Maybe the spilling had been deliberate! Could it be that he had the answers to the diabolical forces at work against me and my aunt? I wanted to question him but dared not. I was just beginning to make inroads on his distrust. How could I gamble that away on some highly unlikely supposition that he knew something? He had been tortured enough by other adults; I could not add to his uneasiness.

Kipp sat by my bed and we held hands and talked. He told me he had gone to Millie's house to ask about her new boarder. "That business about someone being in the cabin worried me. She denied that she had ever seen a woman in a pale green gown. The young brunette is the only new girl she has. I asked her about the woman on the train and she said she didn't know anything about her. She could have been lying to me, but I don't know why. If she has some new wares to strut before customers, she's not bashful."

"But they got on the train together," I protested, "and the girl was handling her baggage. I'm sure of it!"

"Millie says she didn't see her at the station when she picked up the new girl in her carriage. Are you sure she was with them?"

I frowned, trying to remember. "No, I only say a blond woman climbing in the carriage and had a glimpse of the brunette through the window. Maybe someone else picked her up." *Like Lucretia*. She had been there at the station that same night I arrived. She could have whisked the woman into her own carriage before Kipp and I came back to the depot. She could have lied about being there to pick up a package.

Kipp shrugged. "Well, it's not important. Maybe she's somebody's fancy woman and lives somewhere in the hills. She could have wandered into the cabin while I was gone. Once I found that some kids had had a picnic there."

"But I'm sure that it was her glove!" My voice was rising and he soothed me with a kiss.

"It doesn't matter, darling. I promise you I never saw your mysterious lady. Now, let's forget about her and talk about us." He was very persuasive and I gave myself up to enjoying his tender administrations. I'd think about the glove later. I believed him when he said he didn't know who had left it in his cabin. Maybe he was right. It could have been an innocent thing.

The next afternoon I dressed and walked down the hall to my aunt's room. My limbs still felt rubbery but I wanted to fight the deep lassitude that remained in my body from the drug. I found Aunt Esther restlessly pacing up and down, as if some inner compulsion would not allow her to stop for even a minute. I talked to her in a soothing voice, but nothing I said seemed to reach her. Whoever had tried to kill me had done this to her! She had begged me to leave, but now it was too late. Kipp had declared his love for me. Everything else paled as I reveled in the miracle that this man who had captured my heart loved me too. No one could drive me away now.

Later in the afternoon, Lucretia came to see me. She brought me a bouquet of wildflowers and I looked at them carefully, half-expecting there might be some poison ivy among them. We had tea in the small sitting room, and this time I poured. One part of my mind entertained a suspicion that she might have come to finish a job she failed in once before, so I kept my eyes on my cup.

Even as she asked solicitously about my health, I wondered if she were disappointed that I was alive and well instead of a cold body laid out for burial. She could have laced my drink with the deadly drug. She had had the opportunity. Her eagle eyes must have picked up the bemused exchanges between Kipp and me. She had seen us leave through the side door of the barn, and her jealousy could have leapt beyond reason. If that were the case, I thought, she would have had to bring the drug in her recticule for spontaneous use. That didn't seem likely. Whoever tried to kill me had come to the dance with the lethal drug ready . . . waiting for the right opportunity to use it.

"It was a lovely dance," I said evenly to her, carefully watching her reaction. I was foolish enough to think she might give herself away.

"How can you say that, after what happened? The whole affair was ruined!" Her long neck stretched in pure indignation. "It's absolutely appalling! Your aunt's brought bad luck here to this house. Kipp's suffered financial reversals . . . and now you—you've nearly gotten yourself killed twice! You must have some concern for your own well-being, even if you are too selfish to think of others."

"Whatever evil has been running amok in this town was here before I came," I countered. "It started with my uncle's death. I'm more convinced than ever that he was murdered."

"Nonsense. He lost his balance . . . and fell. The doctor said he broke his neck."

"Dr. Yates also said that the blow on his head could have occurred before he fell. I think he was pushed over that ledge by someone who wanted him dead. All the horrid things that happened at the hotel were diabolically planned . . . the vicious attack on my aunt was deliberate. But the harm had already been done by the time I arrived." I set my chin. "I am not the bad-luck omen in this situation."

"You certainly have *not* helped anything or anybody by coming here."

"That's true. But the only harm I have brought is upon myself."

"You have stirred things up, and you can't deny it! If you would just go and take your aunt with you, we could be done with all of this! I don't suppose you've given any more consideration to what we talked about?"

"As a matter of fact, I had made my decision to leave." She brightened. "Not because of your generous offer," I added sarcastically, "but because I could not see that I was needed here. Luckily, the night of the dance, Kipp convinced me otherwise. He loves me and I love him," I said boldly, recklessly throwing our love in her face. I had the satisfaction of seeing those narrow nostrils flare.

"You lied. You said you had no interest in Kipp."

"Yes, I lied . . . but as much to myself as anyone. But now that I trust him—"

Her laugh was without mirth. "Foolish, foolish child. Kipp might have been the faithful lover at one time, but not anymore. Marianne saw to that. He'll dally with you for a while and then toss you aside like all the others. Has he talked of marriage?''

''No, but—''

''I thought not,'' she said with obvious satisfaction. ''He's just enjoying himself. It's really disgraceful, your being here under his roof and all. I was right about you after all. You were trying to feather your nest from the first. You may have come to see your aunt, but don't think your little act of dedication fooled me. I knew the first time I met you at the station that you were an opportunist. A decent girl would worry about her reputation. When he marries again, it will not be on a whim.''

''True. But neither will he marry to form a business relationship,'' I said pointedly, furious that she had implied I was his mistress. ''Kipp will marry for love and companionship.''

''Love,'' she scoffed. ''What an insipid notion, worthy of romantic fools. Marriage demands stronger stuff than poetic murmurings. Both Kipp and I know that. You'll be sorry that you did not take my advice and leave when I offered you help. I really hate to see you hurt.''

''You are too kind, Lucretia, worrying about me the way you do.''

The sarcasm was not lost on her. She stood up, towering over me angrily. ''I hope you can live with yourself . . . and the evil you've brought to this house.'' Then she gave me a tight smile.

"Well, I've had my say. We'll have to wait and see what happens."

We didn't have to wait long. At five o'clock that afternoon, Kipp's new smelter was dynamited and completely destroyed.

I heard the loud boom in the library, where I was reading to Philippe.

"What was that? It sounded like an explosion."

"Sometimes I hear them dynamiting in the mines," he said.

"That didn't sound like it came from the gulch," I commented idly, still not overly concerned. After all, I wasn't accustomed to the sounds of this high mining town. Nothing alerted me that my whole life was going to be changed by that ominous loud boom. I read another page before I heard Tooley yelling as he bounded down the hall from the kitchen.

"The smelter! She's blown!"

"No!" Kipp! Dear God, it couldn't be!

We ran outside to the edge of the promontory.

"There . . ." Tooley gestured, pointing his pudgy finger. "There . . . there . . . see it? I heard the boom, ran out the back door, and there it was—a rising cloud of black smoke!"

"Maybe you're mistaken . . . maybe it's not the smelter," I gasped.

"Same spot it is. You could see the roof just beyond the railroad station. Kipp pointed it out to me the other day. Sure it's the smelter all right. Saints preserve us!"

There was no mistake. Kipp's lovely new building was aflame.

Tooley spun around and ordered Ching Lee to hitch up the buggy.

I didn't wait. I ran to the stable and led Fancy from her stall. My frantic fingers quickly saddled her. I had no time to change into my riding habit, so my navy-blue skirt did not lie smoothly over the saddle horn, but the narrow expanse of my leg showing seemed of little importance. I headed my mount toward the bridle path at reckless speed. *Kipp! Kipp!* He had not come home for lunch. This morning he had kissed me good-bye, excited that the first load of ore was expected at the smelter. *Dear God, in heaven! Let him be safe . . . let him be safe!*

As I passed Lucretia's house, Mary ran to the picket fence. This house didn't have a view of the narrow town as we did from above. She called to me, "What is it? What's happened? I heard an explosion!"

"The smelter," I called back, but did not stop. There was no sign of Lucretia.

As I reached the valley floor, I heard a clanging bell calling the volunteer fire brigade into action. Horses, people, and wagons rushed toward the scene from every direction. Fire could wipe out every building in the town once it was out of control. Fortunately, Kipp had built his smelter down the track from any major building. At the moment I raced toward the mushrooming smoke and fire, I cared little about the safety of property. My selfish anguish was centered on one man. Sparks were flying everywhere. Heat radiated in waves from the inferno.

A red fire wagon with its snorting team

reached the edge of the burning building, and immediately a human line began to form, passing buckets of water up from the creek. The noise was deafening. Whinnying horses and bawling mules added to the cacophony of shouting from the firefighters and cries from frantic people who saw their homes and livelihoods threatened. Fancy was shoved about in the mob like flotsam in a raging current. Her nostrils flared with the scent of smoke and she pawed and jerked in protest as I kicked her forward. Suddenly I was stopped by a burly man who grabbed her reins.

"Get back!"

"Kipp Halstead!" I screamed frantically at him. "Have you seen him?"

"No, but the Doc has someone over at the station. Now, move back, lady, give the firemen room!"

I jerked Fancy's head around and plunged through the milling crowd until I reached the tracks, and then followed them back to the station. I could see a group of men gathered around someone sitting on the ground. It had to be him . . . it had to be! Leaping out of the saddle, I flung Fancy's reins through a hitching ring and ran.

"Kipp?" I sobbed as I pushed through to glimpse the man sitting there, and then stopped. It wasn't Kipp—but Chad. He sat there with his sandy hair and face blackened and his clothes looking as if he'd rolled in the dirt. He looked up at me, the whites of his eyes peering weirdly out of his sooty face.

"Chad!" I fell down beside him. "What happened? Kipp? Where's Kipp?"

He brushed a hand over his eyes. "I was outside getting ready to bring in another car of ore—and she blew! I must have been tossed twenty feet. Found myself lying flat near an abandoned ore car . . . it all happened too fast."

"And Kipp! *Where's Kipp?*"

He blinked with infuriating slowness. "Kipp . . ." His mind seemed as stunned as the rest of him.

"Was he inside? Was Kipp inside the building?" I braced against his answer.

He licked the dirt off his lips. "No . . . gone . . . to Black Hawk, I think."

Tears ran down my cheeks and my shoulders shook with hysterical relief. *He wasn't dead! He wasn't dead . . . he was safe!* At that moment Dr. Yates pushed me aside.

"You all right, Chadwick?"

"Just shook up a bit . . . nothing broken."

"What happened?"

"Must have been dynamite. Somebody set it off in the middle of the smelter. Blew timber in every direction. Knocked me twenty feet, it did. Thank God, I was outside . . . had some protection from some ore cars."

I didn't listen to any more. At the moment I cared about only one thing: Kipp was safe.

It wasn't until I was back at the house that I began to realize what this disaster meant for Kipp. He had sunk everything he had into building the smelter. It was supposed to turn his luck around, to bring him and the town prosperity. And now it was gone. I railed against the injustice of it.

Ching Lee brought Philippe back with him, and Tooley came home hours later, saying the building was leveled but the fire had been contained. He'd been on the water line, passing hundreds of buckets from the creek. The town had been saved from a disastrous fire. The only loss was Kipp's. My heart ached for him.

"Has Kipp come back to town?" I asked Tooley.

"No . . . but someone sent word to Black Hawk. He knows by now," he said sadly.

I waited for him to come, but night came and still there was no Kipp. I paced in the library, my ears tuned to the slightest sound of horse's hooves. Nothing. Only silence that left me alone with my haunting thoughts. Where was he? Was he trying to find the culprit and release his murderous feelings on the one who had destroyed his dreams?

I managed to read some more of *The Last of the Mohicans* to Philippe and then sent him off to bed. Restless and anxious, I did not want to be alone. I found Tooley in the kitchen, sitting at the table with a bottle of whiskey at his elbow. The room reeked of liquor and the glass in his hand must have been filled and emptied several times, for his face was flushed and his eyes were already glazed. Something lost and forlorn deep inside made me sit down across from him.

"Mind if I sit with you? I . . . I don't feel like being by myself."

" 'Tis a sad day, lass . . . a sad day. An

honest man like Kipp doesn't deserve it." He took another drink.

"You love him a lot, don't you?" I said, pouring a cup of coffee from a pot simmering on the front lid of the coal range. None of us had eaten much dinner, and even now my stomach muscles were taut with anxiety.

"And well I should." His eyes narrowed in memory. "Kipp found me dead drunk, lying out in the rain after me wife and son were killed, and he brought me here. They went over the edge . . . stagecoach from Denver City . . . while I was waiting here to welcome 'em. Happy, I was, about starting a new life in this great country. Gone, all gone!" He snapped his fingers. "Just like that. I wanted to die too, but Kipp would have none of it. He sobered me up. Gave me a home, and never a harsh word when I can't fight the demon in me. He's a good man, lass . . . a good man." He peered at me. "But I'm thinking ye know that already."

"Yes, I love him too, Tooley, and my heart is breaking for him." I blew into the lace hankie I kept in my pocket. "I know how much this smelter meant to him. I just can't believe anyone would do such a thing!"

He shook his head again. "A sad day," he repeated, and took another drink.

I left him there, drinking himself into a stupor. Alone once more, I paced the library. *Maybe he hadn't gone to Black Hawk at all. Maybe Chad had been mistaken!* Fear slithered like a snake into my stomach. *Maybe Kipp had been in his office— and no one knew it! He might be lying dead in the rubble!* No, I wouldn't let myself think such crucifying thoughts. He was safe. He had to be. Cold sweat broke out on my brow.

Finally I could not wait any longer. I had to go find him. Maybe he had come back . . . maybe he was trying to assess what damage had been done . . . if anything at all might be saved.

Hurrying upstairs, I changed into my riding habit. The house was quiet, with its usual insidious gloom, and I was glad to leave it. Ching Lee was not in the stables, so once more I saddled Fancy myself and headed down the bridle path.

It was a cloudy night and darkness was all around me as I clutched the reins with moist hands. The valley far below was caught in a swirling blackness like that of a deep pool. A sprinkling of lights like reflected stars broke the murky darkness. One false step from my mount and we would go over the side. I bit my lip and prayed that Fancy was as surefooted as she seemed.

However, my own safety scarcely touched the perimeters of my mind. My all-consuming thought was to find Kipp as soon as possible. He must be back from Black Hawk by now. The whole valley lay in purple-black shadows, but he might still be at the site of the smelter, sifting through rubbish by lanternlight. It did not seem likely—but it was the only idea I had. Then another thought hit me. When we reached the second path jutting off into the woods, I impulsively pulled up the mare. My decision to ride to the smelter site wavered. Fancy sidled impatiently. In a flash of insight I suddenly knew where I would find Kipp. There was one place he would go to find solace, to pull himself together and suffer his defeat alone.

I kicked Fancy lightly and she bolted into the forest. At night, dead trees held out bare limbs, sharp, jagged, and angled like skeleton bones against the sky. The wind moaned restlessly through the arched needled branches while night scavengers scurried away from my mare's thumping hooves. I cried out as a night hawk dived across the path with a whir of wings. Branches whipped dangerously near my face as I hunched down over the mare's neck and let her have her head. Better to trust the mare's instinct to discern the path than try to guide her. She knew where we were going.

The dark tunnel of trees seemed endless. My nerves were raw-edged by the time we reached the small clearing. Then my fright dissipated in one thankful instant.

I had been right.

Feeble lamplight flickered through a small window in the cabin.

14

HE was sitting in the large wing chair, holding his face in his hands. As I came in, he lifted his haggard face and for a moment I felt like an intruder. Then he said my name with such a strangled sob that I flew to his side. He pulled me down on his lap and buried his face in my hair. His chest heaved with sobs. "It's gone . . . every last damned timber . . . burned to the ground!"

Tears flowed down my cheeks. "But you're safe . . . safe . . ." My hands stroked the dark head pressed next to mine. "You could have been killed! Oh, Kipp, darling, don't you see that all that really matters is that you're alive . . . safe? Nothing else is important! I've been frantic with worry." I turned his face to mine and kissed him until the rigidity of his mouth was gone.

"Allie . . . Allie . . ." He held my face gently in his hands and a feeble smile eased the deep clefts in his face. "Thank God for you," he whispered. Deep, dark eyes searched my face.

"I was going to ask you to marry me. Offer you everything I had." His laugh was strained. "And now it seems I have nothing to offer you."

"Only yourself," I said quite boldly, lacing my fingers in his hair. "That's quite enough."

"I may not be able to keep the house."

"You have this cabin . . ."

"You'd be willing to live here?"

"Are you proposing to me, Mr. Kipp Halstead, Esquire?"

He seemed surprised as a sudden rush of new hope surged into his craggy face. "I had decided on an elegant proposal with diamonds and champagne . . . and I was going to do the romantic bit on bended knee and ask you very formally if you would do me the honor of becoming my wife—"

"Yes, I would . . . or will," I stammered, and then laughed foolishly. "If that's a proposal, then I'm accepting . . . without diamonds and champagne."

His eyebrows drew together. "You don't need time to think it over?"

"Not if you truly want *me*, for that's all I have to offer you."

"Want you! My love, you've been like fire in my blood since the first moment I tasted those lips. Having you in the house has been a sweet breath of new life. I never thought it would happen to me again . . . that I would look forward to a new day with such eagerness. I've watched you with my son and have seen you as the mother he should have had. If only . . . But it's too late for all of that. The past is gone, but how can I ask you to start over with me? It wouldn't be fair to you."

"You mean I would have to give up a dull spinster's life for the joy of being needed and loved and cared for by the most handsome, wonderful man in the world?" With mock seriousness I said, "I'm prepared to make the sacrifice. I'll give up my cold dormitory bed for one that offers something more than a quiet night's sleep."

"Why, Miss Allison Lacey, I do believe you're blushing." He buried his face against the softness of my breasts. "If you only knew how many times I wanted to come and share your bed. The torture of knowing you were just a few steps across the hall . . ."

"I know. I lay there listening . . . lecturing myself about letting you in. But I wanted to be in your arms like this."

Words were lost as pent-up desire flowed between us with the swiftness of an open spillgate. We kissed hungrily and held each other as if the only reality lay in the radius of our embrace. There was a soaring sweetness that was gentle yet aggressive as his hands traced the soft mounds of my breasts and brought a delicious tingling to the tips of my hardened nipples. I made no protest when he swung me up in his arms and carried me into the small bedroom. In the folds of the soft feather bed, he lazily undressed me, trailing kisses over my bare skin, arousing a delicious explosion of sensory buds.

In another moment he was beside me under

the soft quilt and I turned into the sweet length of his chest, hips, and legs. I had never known intimacy with a man, but already my body knew a hungering for my lover's touch. I was aroused, excited, and frightened too.

"It's all right, love," he soothed. "Just let the pleasure grow and swell and spread to every tingling, delicious part of your luscious body."

He kissed my breasts and one hand slid gently downward until his palm pressed with slow rhythm against the soft mound between my legs. I did not know what was happening to me but it was not a frightening thing, for he took me slowly, with tantalizing sureness. Caught up in the bewildering delight, I felt myself growing moist and warm and ready to receive him. My short cry of pain mingled with his breath as it was suddenly shut off by his kiss. When he entered me, the pulsating rhythm of our bodies held a familiarity that was definitive of a glorious expression of love. A spiral of passion took me upward in a wild burning ecstasy until the glorious sensation fragmented and I cried out in amazement.

He cradled me against him and slowly I floated down from the heights of physical enchantment. "My wonderful, beautiful love," he whispered. "My own dear Allie."

I smiled happily. The world could not intrude upon me at that moment. I cared not that I had flaunted conventions and loved this man before the marriage vows were said. The miracle that I had found him was too wondrous to be denied. A blessed lassitude, like a floating magic carpet, carried me as I lay with my head against his chest and marveled that his firm, warm flesh had been a part of me.

We talked then, not about the present, for both of us were eager to know about the other—our childhoods, the dreams we'd dreamed, and the unmet longings to find the right person to share our lives. Loneliness had been with us both, and now it was gone. We kissed, made love again, and wondered at the whole feeling that suddenly diminished the rest of the world. I snuggled cozily against him and would have remained with him all night if he hadn't kissed me awake a little later and insisted that he get me back to the house before everyone was astir.

"They might be worried about you. We don't want Tooley to raise a posse," he said as he reluctantly eased from the bed and slipped on his trousers. Moonlight coming through the small window flickered upon his chest and touched the strong contours of his face. I felt a strange lump in my throat as I realized this virile man was mine. He would share my bed for all the nights of my life. I gave a soft giggle of wanton anticipation.

"What are you snickering about?" Playfully he gave the quilt a quick pull and cold air rushed upon my bare skin. I squealed a protest but delighted in the appreciative gleam in his eyes as they stroked my nakedness. "You have one second to dress, or suffer the consequences," he ordered.

"And if you don't put on a shirt, neither of

us will have a choice," I warned in the same capricious tone.

He hesitated as if he were going to test my challenge, but then he shook his head regretfully, his eyes sparkling. "You sorely test me, but I must get you back to the house."

As I dressed, he sat on the edge of the bed and began to talk about the explosion. "If I ever catch the bastard—"

"It wasn't an accident, then?"

"No. Couldn't have been. There wasn't anything in the mill to make an explosion like that. It was deliberately set, all right. Must have been a whole box of dynamite . . . placed right in the middle of the building."

"But who? Who would do such a vicious thing?"

"Someone who wants to ruin me. Thank God, there weren't any workers around yet . . . just Chad."

"He wasn't hurt, just badly shaken," I said.

"I left him to handle some of the ore cars while I went to Black Hawk to see when more would be arriving. Someone must have waited until he went outside and then set the charge. If I'd been there—"

"Thank heavens, you weren't!"

"If I had been, I might have been able to stop it. Someone doesn't want me to recoup my financial losses. Well, the sonofabitch succeeded."

"You'll start again. I know you will. There are things in the house . . . you could sell them," I began, thinking I was offering hope.

He looked at me with such constricted anguish that I wished I'd never mentioned the house. "And after it's gone . . . then what? This cabin? No, it will never end . . . not until some bastard is satisfied that there's nothing left."

"We have to find out who it is."

"Don't you think I've done everything I possibly could to find out? My efforts have been for naught. I haven't been able to get even a glimmer of who is behind these treacherous acts. My God, I've been going crazy thinking about the danger you've been in since you came here. And Esther! Who is responsible for such malevolence against her? I took her into my house for her own protection—"

"Maybe that's why this happened to you. Oh, Kipp, I'll never forgive myself if my family has brought this upon you. Lucretia warned me—"

"Damn Lucretia. I wish she'd keep her nose out of my business."

"But maybe she was right."

"I don't know what in the hell to think anymore!"

"Who would gain by all this? Don't they always say you have to look for the motive in any crime? Who would profit by financially ruining my aunt and you? What are they after?"

"Maybe they're not after anything. Maybe they're just insane."

"I don't think so. Everything that has happened has been cunningly executed, as if according to some diabolical plan. I think my arrival complicated things, but I don't know how. Unless . . ."

How could I tell him how jealous Lucretia was of his attentions toward me? Would she do such a terrible thing to a man she obviously wanted to marry? I thought her capable of such treachery, but my suspicions might be my own personal aversion to her. But I couldn't hold back the question. "Do you think Lucretia could be trying to ruin you . . . make you financially dependent on her?"

His heavy black eyebrows raised. "Lucretia? Don't be ridiculous. She and Tim were the only friends I had in this country when I didn't know whether or not I was going to be able to last out the next winter. If we hadn't hit with the Goldstock mine, none of us would have left here with more than worn-out shoes and a knapsack. Lucretia has a good business head—better than mine, it appears. She tried to talk me out of putting money in your aunt's hotel—"

"But you bought it anyway. Why?" Even now the sore festered that he had taken my aunt's hotel from her.

"I didn't exactly buy it. I loaned Esther money to try to keep afloat when things went bad. You see, your Uncle Benjamin was a prince of a fellow, honest, hardworking, and a real asset to a growing town like Glen Eyrie. I hated to see his widow lose everything. Your aunt and uncle had borrowed heavily from the bank to make all the improvements, but before they finished,

Benjamin was killed and nasty things happened at the hotel to ruin its business. Anyway, your aunt deeded me half of the hotel to keep the bank's hands off it, but she still owns the other half."

"So you're really partners," I said in a rush of relief.

"Yes . . . partners in a closed-up hotel that isn't worth the ground it's setting on."

"But why . . . why didn't you tell me that in the beginning?"

"I didn't know anything about you . . . I thought you might be here just to get what you could from Esther. It seemed best to pretend that she didn't have any more interest in the hotel. I was wrong about you, of course . . . and I apologize. It seems that I've not been very smart about a lot of things. I'm not sure that Esther doesn't resent me now. Her behavior indicates that she thinks I'm responsible for what's happened. That's what you've been thinking, isn't it? Oh, I could tell that you had me all set up for the culprit. At least now you know someone else is responsible. I wouldn't sabotage my own smelter." His smile was wan.

I couldn't lie to him. I had been torn apart by my suspicions while falling hopelessly in love with him. But now that conflict was over. I put my arms around his neck. "Whoever it is . . . they'll have to fight the two of us now."

"Maybe we should leave Glen Eyrie," he whispered, holding me close.

"You mean, run away?" I chided. "We Laceys are made of stronger stuff than that. Now, let's get back to the house before one of us starts taking off his clothes again."

"Don't bribe me with such promises or we'll never leave." He kissed me long and possessively, then sighed.

Reluctantly we left the cabin, still warm with remembered passion.

15

WE slipped into the house and parted at the top of the stairs. "Off with you, my love," he whispered, nuzzling against my neck. "Once the conventions are observed, we'll never sleep apart."

With that promise ringing in my ears, I hurriedly undressed and slipped into the large bed, already aching for the feel of those engulfing arms and the passionate heat of his body. I thought I was too keyed-up to sleep, but I must have slipped away into a sound slumber because I heard nothing the rest of the night. SuLang's hand roughly shaking my shoulder, awoke me at dawn.

"Wh-what?" I stammered, befuddled as I rose out of thick layers of sleep to see her bending over my bed. Unbidden, panic surged through me and brought me upright. "What . . . what is it?"

"Miss Esther . . . she not in her room! Where Miss Esther go?" Her tone was accusing, as if I had somehow whisked my aunt away without her knowledge. "I check on her before I go downstairs this morning. She's not in her bed."

"Oh, dear, she's probably wandering around the house again." I grabbed my wrapper and slipped my feet into my soft slippers. "Check the rest of the rooms on this floor . . . I'll go downstairs. The doors were locked last night. She couldn't have gotten out." I gave SuLang a weak reassuring smile. I knew that Kipp had locked the doors behind us when we came back about one o'clock. I had peeked in on Aunt Esther before blowing out my lamp; she had been sound asleep then. As I hurried downstairs, an uneasiness which defied analysis dried all the moisture from my mouth. Some primeval instinct brought shivers that had nothing to do with the early-morning hours.

The lower hall was clammy and cold. Like ghostly specters, the first early light of the day was wafting through the entry windows. I checked the library first, hoping to see Aunt Esther sitting in one of the large leather chairs with that vacant smile on her face. But the room was hauntingly empty.

A sense of urgency rose in me even though one part of my mind continued to reassure myself that nothing could have happened to her inside the house with all the doors locked. My nightdress and pelisse wrapper whispered along the floor as I returned to the foyer and started down the hall toward the lived-in part of the house. A slight crack of light under the parlor door caught my eye and stopped me.

I had passed this closed room a hundred times

since that first night I had stepped inside it, but the memory of its disconcerting, almost evil coldness always hastened my steps past it. Even now, as I paused in front of the door, my hand trembled as I reached for the doorknob. As the crack widened, I braced myself against the waiting, brooding atmosphere of the gray, shadow-laced room. Like a repetitious dream of chilling quality, its elegant furniture and heavy drapings were reflected as obscure images in the dusty mirrors. A faint tinkle of the huge chandelier above me defined a movement of unseen air. An unnamed but horrible aura seemed to be emitted from the very walls. It was real, almost palatable. It had been here waiting, and I felt the touch of death even before I saw her crumpled body.

My scream reverberated to the high ceiling of the room. I threw myself down beside her, knowing once more that I had come too late. Aunt Esther's head lay at a crooked angle. This time the assault had been sure and deadly. A bloody brass candlestick from the dusty mantel lay beside her crushed skull. Her body was still slightly warm as I gathered her to me and wept hysterically.

Hands pulled me away as I sobbed uncontrollably. Kipp carried me out of the room as SuLang knelt beside Aunt Esther, wailing and wringing her hands. He laid me on a sofa in the sitting room, holding me close, hushing my cries with soft murmurings. His voice poured over me but I could not fasten onto the meaning of his words. My aunt was dead! Thoughts like barbed pellets, cutting and wounding, were recalled from her frantic letters to this horrid moment. The first attempt on her life had failed, but the fiend who wanted her dead had not given up. I cried for the woman she had been before disaster overtook her, and grieved that I had come too late. At last my sobs slackened and I raised my tear-filled eyes to Kipp's. I saw then that his face was ashen too, and his eyes moist. This murderous invasion of his house had shaken and appalled him. My lover's shattered expression reached me through my grief and I pulled his head against my chest and comforted him. "What are we going to do?" I said in a strangled whisper.

Last night I had been blasé about finding out who was behind the treachery, but I knew now that a murderer would not be content until we were all dead . . . even Kipp! "We must leave here," I sobbed. "You were right. We must go away . . . now . . . today!"

He raised his head and his jaw tightened as his hands settled firmly on my shoulders. "Yes, darling . . . you must go. I can't take any more chances. You must wait in Denver City—"

"No, I'm not leaving without you!"

"For God's sake, Allie, I can't take any more! You've been in danger ever since you got here. I can't protect you! My house isn't safe anymore—even with locks on the door!"

"But . . . but how could anyone get in?"

"I don't know! You saw me lock up when we came in."

"But there was no one in the house except

Tooley, Philippe, SuLang, and maybe Ching Lee. Tooley was drinking heavily when I left, and Philippe had already gone off to bed. Maybe someone came after I left?"

"Tooley must really be stoned if your shrieks didn't awaken him. Will you be all right? I'll check on him and Philippe and send Ching Lee for Dr. Yates."

I nodded. Blessed numbness was coating the horror, nature's way of deadening shock. My mind and body were held in a kind of suspension. "I'll get dressed," I said, as if that were the most important consideration at the moment.

"Yes . . . maybe we'd both better get out of our nightclothes." He put his arm around my shoulders and led me from the room, tightening his grip as he guided me quickly past the parlor. The door was closed now and I assumed SuLang had disappeared into some private corner to assuage her own grief.

I dressed carefully, like one braced for pain, as if waiting for something nebulous, with a holding of my breath. Looking back, I think I knew that the nightmare had not fully unfolded. Apprehension hovered around me like a formless black cloud. The house was charged with a tension that threatened to snap like summer lightning. I heard Kipp going down the stairs, and had just finished buttoning my light gray frock and twisting my hair severely at the back of my head when I heard him racing back up, calling my name.

"Allie!"

"What is it?" I ran to him. My heart leapt into

213

my throat and stopped beating. I knew from his face that the horror had just begun.

"Philippe . . . he's gone," he croaked. "He must have been taken from his bed sometime during the night!"

I don't know how I got through the hours of that day without giving way to hysterics. It was Kipp's need that kept me rational as the search began. I kept hoping that Philippe was just playing one of his malicious tricks.

"Maybe he ran away."

"In the middle of the night?"

"We don't know when it happened. Tooley was dead drunk. Philippe could have heard me screaming this morning," I offered, "and left the house in fright. He'll be back, I know he will." There must be a reasonable explanation. I clung to the hope that someone would find him at any moment of that long day, but raw fear grew with every passing hour.

Tooley confessed that he had drunk himself into a stupor. He blamed himself for everything that had happened. " 'Twas my weakness and self-pity that made me worthless when I was needed. If the boy comes back safe, I swear by my sainted mother, another drop will never pass my lips!" Tears came into those round eyes and I knew nothing I could say would lessen the anguish he was feeling.

"But how did they get in? The doors were locked."

"Aye, and still locked they be this morning."

"Then who . . . ?"

"Someone with a key. It had to be."

The only name that came to my mind was Lucretia's. I must find out if Kipp had given her a key to the house.

Aunt Esther's body was taken away and prepared for burial. Word had been sent to Reverend Gilly that he was needed to officiate at services as soon as possible. With one part of my brain I tried to take care of all the necessary details and keep the house running. SuLang had disappeared and Ching Lee said she had gone to be with friends in Black Hawk. I was glad to have her gone. Her reproachful eyes were too much for me to bear at the moment. She had loved my aunt with fanatical devotion and my heart was saddened that she had lost her surrogate mother.

Kipp had put out the word that his son was missing, and volunteers began to ride the gulches and search the numerous open mines in the district. If Philippe were wandering around the area, he would be found.

My only peace lay in activity. I had to keep busy or my anxiety and grief would now engulf me. I could not stay in the house.

I asked Ching Lee to saddle Fancy for me. It was foolish to think that I might discover something that others had missed, but I had to do something besides stay in that brooding house that had rejected me from the moment I entered the door. It was like a living thing; cold, unfriendly.

I took Fancy and rode into the band of aspen trees where Philippe had led me that first day.

215

The stand of quaking aspens were in full bloom now, quivering and twisting on their stems, sending flickering shadows across the forest floor. Their white trunks gave way to dense stands of pine and spruce which crowded down from the higher slopes. I did not know if I could find my way to the lip of the precipice where I had fallen, but some weird intuition led me there. I did not believe that Philippe had left the house voluntarily, and the thought that he was in the clutches of some demented person was more than I could bear. Although I tried to ignore it, one insidious thought would not let me rest.

Could he have killed Aunt Esther and then fled from the house?

It was possible that she had come upon him in the midst of some mischief. Not knowing that in her mental state she could not harm him, he either threw the candlestick or struck her with it. It was possible that he had acted in haste—or was manipulated by someone. I had felt more than once that someone was deliberately poisoning his mind, but lately he had come around so beautifully that I was certain I had been mistaken. Now I wondered.

I had gone with Kipp to the boy's room to look for any hint as to what might have happened. There was no sign of struggle . . . and his play clothes from the day before were gone! Either he had grabbed them up and left in his nightclothes, or someone had taken him and the clothes. If Tooley hadn't been dead drunk across the hall, surely he would have heard Philippe leave.

As Fancy threaded her way through the heavy underbrush, these speculations were as grim as the choking juniper and mahogany shrubs tangling my legs and tearing at my skirts.

"Philippe! Philippe!" My voice bounded away into the dark depths of the forest and was lost in a rustle of arching needled branches. I reined the mare around fallen logs already host to termites and beetles. Several times furry creatures darted out from their hollow centers. In this claustrophobic tangle of vines, stalks, and trunks, Philippe could have been lying only a foot away and I would have passed him unnoticing. Frustration and anxiety blurred my vision. "Philippe . . . Philippe," I croaked, my voice threaded with desperation. I knew then how much I had come to love the child. He was precious to me, not only because he was a part of Kipp but also because he had so nearly been mine to love and raise.

I could not find my way out of the neverending trees. My resolve to return to the spot where Philippe had led me deserted me. How foolish I had been to come this way. I should have gone along the ridge, the way Kipp had led his horse back to the house that day.

I reined Fancy around on a narrow patch of soft moss and prayed I could find my way back. Kipp would be furious if I added to his worries by becoming lost. I patted Fancy's neck and wondered if I should trust her judgment. It seemed the wise thing to do, but a short time later I realized how trusting I had been, for she took me directly to a small stream I had never seen before. Could it be the same one that ran behind Kipp's cabin? As Fancy bent her head and drank in the clear, swift creek, I decided that following it downward was the best safeguard against becoming hopelessly lost. If I were correct, this was Minute Creek, whose tumbling waters I had heard during my visits to the cabin.

Following a little stream was not the simple task I had imagined. It cut through tiny faults which were scarcely wide enough for Fancy to squeeze through, and often its banks held slippery rocks that had tumbled from above. As her hooves slid off rocks and clattered against the hard stone, I prayed she would not sprain an ankle. I knew then that Lucretia had been right. A novice rider in these mountains could only come to harm.

Several times I got off and led the mare down steep inclines that threatened to tumble us both to our knees. Then I would have to find a log or rock to act as a mounting block so I could climb on her again. My riding habit was torn and the hem wet and muddy from swishing along the edges of the water. The streamers on my hat had been ripped off by a dead twig that had snared it when I ducked under an overhanging branch.

I despaired that the creek was leading me farther and farther away from any familiar terrain. Unexpectedly, Fancy lifted her head and neighed. I could see nothing but more trees and rocks. She pulled at the reins, so I let her have her head. She came out of a band of trees that hid the small corral and the cabin from view! I would have ridden right past it if she hadn't alerted me to its presence.

I tethered Fancy and went inside. Everything was just as we had left it. Had it been only last night when Kipp had proposed to me and we made love in that wondrous feather bed? How could such happiness have been wrenched away from us so brutally? Could someone have known I was here with him and deliberately followed us back to the house to wreak vengeance?

The idea would not leave me. I looked out a small window. Thick stocks of pussywillow bushes outside the bedroom made a tight hedge down to the creek. Anyone could have been a few feet from the cabin and escaped notice. Even now, I could not tell if I was truly alone.

It was possible that someone had seen me arrive at the cabin and then followed us back to the main house, waiting until slumber was upon us before committing murder and kidnapping. I could not understand why anyone would hate us so.

I stepped out on the small stoop of the cabin and looked around, searching for a formless face lurking in the shadow that would answer all my questions. I was not afraid. My hands clenched. I wanted something tangible to rail against. I willed the unseen evil to show itself.

Nothing. My imaginings were folly. Nothing stirred, no human form emerged to take up my challenge. I was alone.

Weary and despondent, I mounted Fancy and took the bridle path back up the mountain to the house. Green-black shadows spread a possessive mantle across the promontory as we reached the ridge behind the house. No color brightened the somber backdrop of conifiers except . . .

I reined in Fancy. She pawed restlessly, protesting this stop when we were in sight of the barn. My eyes fixed on it—a patch of green, as pale as an aspen leaf, fluttering in the bush at the top of the bridle path. Its translucent sheen was visible only because of the darker contrast of the bush.

It drew me like a magnet—the filmy green net of a lady's hat!

16

I held the scrap of netting in my hand. First a glove and now this! My heart began to race. Kipp had dismissed the mystery lady as having no importance in the present circumstances, but I was convinced now that she had been in the cabin—and now here just above the bridle path!

I could hardly wait to show it to Kipp. The day wore on into evening, and then into night. Finally he came with a group of searchers carrying lanterns. His broad shoulders were slumped and the proud lift of his head had disappeared. Deep lines etched worry on his drawn face, and dark circles under his eyes showed a lack of sleep. I wondered if Philippe would ever know how much his father really loved him.

In the privacy of the library I showed him the piece of green netting. "I found it behind the house, caught in the bushes," I said anxiously, watching his face.

He turned it over in his hands, perplexed. "What is it?"

"It's netting from a lady's hat—the kind I saw

the mystery lady wearing. Don't you see, it proves she was here . . . as well as at the cabin."

"Allie, this cloth could have blown in from anywhere," he said wearily. "I think you're letting your imagination run away with you. I know you're trying to help, but I don't have time to work this out now. I have to go. We're going downstream as far as the lake. Philippe's been there several times with Tooley catching frogs. I don't know where else to look. What could have happened to him?" His voice broke. I put my arms around him and he held me close. We both drew strength from the embrace. "I'm afraid, Allie." His voice shook. Those haunted deep-set eyes probed my face. "Be here for me, Allie . . . promise?"

"I will . . . I will."

"I couldn't stand up to this alone. Not now— not when I've found you. If you left—"

"Hush." I let my hands trace the deep lines along his cheeks, then put my face against his. "I love you. Whatever happens, we'll face it together."

He straightened his shoulders and went out to the men waiting in the stableyard. I heard the sound of horses' hooves fade away, leaving the house silent and brooding.

They'll find him safe. They have to! I remained in the library. It was the only room in the house where I could feel Kipp's presence . . . and Philippe's. I looked at those smudged cards, so painfully lettered and carefully arranged amid the rock specimens. *The Last of the Mohicans* lay on the table waiting for our next reading. I covered my face with my hands and cried.

Tooley and I kept a vigil for most of the night, catching fitful naps as we waited for the search party to return. Morning came and no message arrived. The nightmare continued and my despair grew with every passing moment.

About midafternoon of the next day, Chad arrived. I could tell from his face that he had some news. His freckled face lacked his usual easygoing grin. Those clear hazel eyes were narrowed. He looked like a stranger instead of my fun-loving partner at the barn dance.

"What is it?" I grabbed his arm as he came into the house. "Have they found him? Is he . . . ?" I choked.

"No. They haven't found him. But there was a note . . . left for Kipp at the bank. Philippe's been kidnapped. They want fifty thousand dollars' ransom!"

"Ransom?" I could not handle this unexpected answer. "Kidnapped?" It took several seconds for the word to have meaning. "But . . . but Kipp doesn't have fifty thousand dollars. Are you sure it isn't a trick?" I had heard of cases where the parents of a lost child were cruelly exploited; someone claiming to have the child would send this kind of note and then disappear with the ransom.

Chad shifted uncomfortably and looked at the tip of his work shoe. "There was a piece of his hair in the letter. Kipp's at the bank now. Maybe he'll be able to borrow the money, if he decides to pay—"

"Of course he'll pay, if that will bring Philippe back safely."

Chad didn't meet my eyes. "I've heard things . . . that he and his son haven't been exactly close, some talk that he even dislikes the boy . . ." He seemed embarrassed to be repeating gossip.

"That's not true! He loves Philippe. If it is at all possible, he'll raise the money."

"Well, then, I guess there's no need for you to worry," he said, relieved. "It's going to be all right. Kipp will tough things out."

"But what . . . what if they don't give him back . . . what if Philippe's already dead!" I sobbed. Someone had killed my aunt, probably the same vicious hands that had snatched Philippe. I wondered if my aunt had somehow interfered with the kidnapping. Maybe her death had not been planned. My head whirled with this bewildering new complication.

"Got to hope for the best," Chad said, trying to soothe me. "Now, try not to worry. I've got to get back, run some more errands for Kipp. He's only got twenty-four hours to come up with the money."

Twenty-four hours. Where would he get the money? All his resources had gone to build the smelter. He would have to mortgage this house and all its contents. Maybe the hotel would bring in a little. We had found my aunt's will, leaving me her half, so now Kipp and I were partners. We could put it up for sale and he could have my half if it would help. With all these unresolved matters whirling in my brain,

I waited for Kipp. But he did not come home that night.

At breakfast Tooley said, "Ye've got to be eating something. It's two days since a decent morsel of food has passed yer lips."

"I . . . I'm not hungry." I covered my face and he clumsily patted my back. "There now, lass, 'tis no good tearing yerself up like this. Ye got to have faith. Kipp'll find him . . . you'll see."

"What if he can't raise the money?"

"Don't ye be worrying about that. If the bank won't give it to him, there's always Mrs. Poole. Sure and she's been wanting to get her hands on this house for a long time."

A cold chill went down my back. "You mean she's tried to buy it from Kipp?"

"Offered him a nice price, and herself included, I'm a-thinkin'." He winked at me with bloodshot eyes. "From what Kipp tells me, he has someone else in mind, and I couldn't be happier. Warms me heart to think of you being a mom to Philippe. Sure and 'tis time Kipp found himself a bonny colleen—'Too good for the likes of you,' I told him." He peered at me. "I'll be leaving with the best of wishes for all of ye."

"Leaving!"

" 'Tis leaving I am . . . right after the wedding."

"But why? Please, Tooley, don't go! We need you!"

" 'Tis nice of ye to be saying so, but ye don't know what ye'd be letting yerself in fer—a drunk who can't be depended upon to boil water . . .

a blurry-eyed cook with a hangover . . . or dead-out when he's in his cups.''

I grabbed his hand and squeezed it. "I'll take you drunk or sober.''

He shook his head. "A mistress of the house won't be putting up with that kind of shenanigans for long. 'Tis best I go before hard feelings set in. No woman wants the likes of me in her kitchen—''

"I do! Oh, Tooley, I do. This is your home. Please don't leave. We love you—all of us! You're family!''

His round eyes were moist. " 'Tis . . . 'tis . . . warming me old heart . . . to be wanted, but I can't be promising anything. 'Tis the devil's urge that comes over me sometimes.''

"I'll take you drunk or sober, Tooley. I couldn't begin to prepare the kind of meals you do. You can't leave. Heaven knows, I'm going to need all the help I can get with this house. It's so . . .'' I involuntarily shivered.

"I know what ye mean. She left her mark on it, Marianne did. It reeks of unhappiness. But now that ye're here, all of that will change.''

"It . . . it hasn't so far,'' I said, bringing us back to the nightmare of Philippe's abduction.

Later that morning I rode to the cabin to see if Kipp had come back there for a few hours' rest. It was empty. I went back to the house. By midafternoon I sent Ching to town to find out what he could. Chad had said that Kipp must pay the ransom in twenty-four hours. The time was up! Would Kipp come back with Philippe

. . . or had he failed to meet the demands? Ching Lee came back and shook his head. "Nobody see him since yesterday. He not in town. Gone."

"Gone where?"

"Nobody say. I sorry. What I do now?"

"I don't know. I guess we'll just have to wait." Anger spilled through my worry. How could Kipp keep me in the dark like this? Was he still trying to raise the money? What would happen to Philippe if he missed the deadline? Had he failed to come up with the ransom—or had he gone to deliver it? I wished now I had asked Chad exactly what the note said. Where was Kipp supposed to take the money?

Maybe Lucretia knew! Sharing these unanswered questions with her would be better than remaining in this clammy, silent house. I couldn't stand the waiting any longer.

"Please saddle my mare, Ching Lee." I needed to be with someone, even someone as abrasive as Lucretia.

There were still three hours of daylight left as the sun headed downward behind the high pointed peaks of the mountain range. The bowl of the sky was a deepening blue with a few clouds waiting to collect the brassy colors of a sunset. I saw no sign of rain, and the wind seemed to have ceased its restless meanderings. The streamers of my hat fluttered from the mare's rhythmic movement and not from any breeze. The stillness of the hillside and of the quiet layered houses below was a sharp contrast to my churning emotions. Inside my breast a tempest raged. How could the outward world be so serene when my personal life was exploding into such chaos?

As I passed the spot where I had found the piece of netting, all the tangled questions came back and I wondered if I had been right about it. Kipp had dismissed it as unimportant, but some nagging intuition told me he was wrong. A disloyal thought made me question whether or not he was keeping something from me. Maybe I would ask Lucretia if she had seen the woman who had come up on the train. Lucretia had been there—collecting a package, she said. But once more I asked: Was it really a package? Or a person?

My imagination ran so furiously along these lines that I was almost prepared to find the veiled lady sitting on Lucretia's veranda when I arrived. With my usual impulsiveness I was prepared to challenge Lucretia about her part in these horrid affairs, forgetting that whoever had perpetrated them was ready to kill again.

I tethered Fancy's reins and strode purposefully up to the front door. Anxiety, anger, frustration, and determination were all in my knock as I banged the lion's-head knocker against the door. I braced myself to meet those arctic green eyes. Instead a pair of merry hazel eyes brightened as the door swung open. Mary, her chubby face creased with a welcoming smile, stepped back and let me enter.

"I wondered if . . . if I might see Mrs. Poole for a few minutes," I said, giving a quick glance into the library. Her desk was vacated and the top of it was neat with stacked books and papers. A quill pen remained in an inkwell waiting for her return.

"I'm sorry, ma'am, she's not here."

"Do you know where I might find her?"

"No, ma'am. Would you like to wait? It's sorry I am to hear about your aunt . . . and the boy. Is there any news?" Her eyes searched mine and I saw sincere concern written there.

"No, and I was hoping that maybe Mrs. Poole had some. Has Mr. Halstead been here, do you know?"

"Yes, ma'am," she said, her face brightening. "This morning, it was. He and the mistress were talking together in the library." Then she glanced around in a conspirator's manner. "I couldn't help but hear . . . me having to dust the hall an' all." I knew Mary's curiosity had vented itself in eavesdropping. "It was the ransom . . . the bank wouldn't loan any more money . . . so he offered his house to the mistress and she agreed to buy it at his price. But he kept back all the furnishings," she said in satisfaction, as if pleased to have her mistress thwarted in something.

I was sick to my stomach. So Lucretia had gotten what she wanted, after all. But Kipp must have come up with the ransom! "Do you know where he was to take the money?" I asked, ashamed to be pumping her like this, but desperate to know what was happening.

"No, ma'am. They didn't say anything about

that, but they left here to go to the bank to get the money. Maybe they would know something there . . . ?"

"Thank you, Mary, very much. You've been a help."

"How is Tooley doing? He's so fond of the boy. Something like this will send him back to the bottle." She sighed. "Such a fine man. If only . . ."

"He says he's going to try to do better," I said impulsively. Maybe something good would come out of all this if Philippe were found safe, I thought. It was obvious Mary cared for Tooley. If only he could put the tragic loss of his first family behind him and let a loving woman like Mary and some healthy, bouncing children ease away his loneliness. As I turned away, my thoughts sped away in another direction. I stopped. "Could you tell me, Mary, if Mrs. Poole has had a houseguest, a lady who wears pale green clothes?"

Mary shook her head. "We never have guests in the house, ma'am. My mistress isn't social. Doesn't entertain—only Mr. Halstead. He's the only one who comes to dinner sometimes."

"I see." Nothing added up the way I expected. "Well, thank you. You've been helpful." I smiled at her. "I'll stop at the bank and see if they have any news."

"Good luck, miss." Then she impulsively touched my arm. "Tooley says you're a very nice lady. I hope everything works out for you."

"Thank you, Mary. And I hope everything

works out for you." We smiled at each other, two women worried about the men they loved.

The only time I had ridden across town had been in a carriage. As Fancy navigated the narrow streets amid mules, buggies, darting children, laborers, and swaggering men with cigars in their mouths, I knew it had been a mistake to come like this. Dust rising from the rutted street clogged my nostrils and put a gritty layer on my teeth. I thought I knew where the stone bank was, but I must have turned one street too soon, for I missed King and found myself on that street Chad had taken that day after church.

Even though dusk was a couple of hours away, women were already leaning in narrow doorways seductively, as if expecting the first wave of customers for the night. Bare shoulders, enticing décolleté necklines, and peeping ankles were boldly displayed for the passersby. Several jeered at me as I rode past. "Are you looking for some business, girlie?" Their raucous laughter followed me down the street.

With as much poise as my thumping heart would allow, I passed the crib shacks, but when I reached Millie's large gingerbread house, I couldn't help but let my glance search the premises for Kipp's black horse. He might have come to Millie to borrow money, I thought. She and Lucretia might be the ones who would give him a loan when the bank refused. I knew he would put aside all pride to get his son back. If only I had the nerve to walk up to the door and find out from Millie what was happening.

But I couldn't! Kipp would be appalled by

such behavior. He had already asked Millie about my mystery lady, and she had told him her new boarder was the small brunette girl. But I could not let go of the possibility that the veiled woman had also been in Millie's carriage that night at the station. I didn't know why the madam would lie to Kipp, but the glimpse I'd had of the woman indicated she was as tough as the business she was in.

The winding street finally led me to the center of town and the stone bank. Dismounting, I left Fancy at a hitching rail and hurried across the boardwalk to the front door with the gold lettering that read "Halstead Bank." The name was a mockery to all the losses Kipp had suffered. Once, he had been the principal stockholder, and now they had refused him an adequate loan to ransom his son. Every time Kipp lost something, Lucretia gained. She would have his house now, and if the hotel had been worth anything, she'd have had it by now too.

I pulled on the doorknob before I read the sign. Bank hours were from nine to three. It was already half-past four. Tears of frustration stung my eyes as I turned away. Listlessly I went back to my mare and mounted again. I did not know where to go. As I lifted my head I saw the tiny steeple of the little church across the gulch. Reverend Gilly had sent word he would be here on Sunday to bury Aunt Esther in the small cemetery where Uncle Benjamin had been laid to rest. I kicked Fancy in a slow trot up the hill and we passed the Lacey Hotel. It stood there deserted, overgrown with weeds, pathetic with neglect. Once it had been a prosperous Victorian hotel, but someone had brought about its ruin.

It's the hotel! Aunt Esther had screamed at me that night.

Her frantic voice echoed in my ears. "It's the hotel," I said aloud. What did she mean by that? I had not been back since that first day when Kipp had emerged from his office and taken me in his arms. Office! Maybe he was there . . . or maybe there was some clue as to where he had gone. I knew that luckily he had not had time to move everything to the smelter before it was destroyed.

New hope made me kick Fancy into a trot. I left her in front of the hotel and hurried around to the side door. This time it was locked, so I went around the back to the door I had seen leading into Kipp's office. Timber, rocks, and piled dirt left by my uncle's remodeling project almost blocked my way. Picking my way around the refuse, I finally reached the door and found it unlocked. The room was as it had been before. Disappointment assailed me.

Perhaps I expected to see Kipp sitting at his magnificent English desk, his dark head bent over the money he had collected, his cane resting nearby and a glass of brandy near his inkwell. The empty room was as haunting as the house I had left.

A fusty, stale smell greeted me and I knew he had not been here for some time. Gray ashes lay stone cold in the fireplace. I let my gloved hand run along the dusty surfaces of the small table between the two chairs. Here I had sat that first day—and thrown my brandy in his face. I closed my eyes against a rush of emotion. Kipp . . . Kipp. His name was a prayerful incantation on my lips. How could I survive if something happened to him? My life had been empty and sterile until I came to Glen Eyrie and experienced the heights and depths of loving. It was too late to go back to the prim, innocent Allison who had never known the rush of passion through her veins or let her senses soar in a lovers' embrace.

I clenched my fists against a rising swell of despair. I opened the door into the dark hall. This was the spot where I had first seen him. Ahead, at the end of the hall, afternoon light came through dirty windows of the lobby, touching the discarded furniture and barren floor with an eerie patina. I moved toward the huge room. How I wished I could have seen it alive with people, heard resounding laughter and music rising to the high beamed ceiling. My aunt and uncle had put so much of themselves into the hotel, their hard work, their dreams that the Lacey Hotel would be the most fashionable in the high Rockies. In my mind's eye I could see the mirrored lobby, silk and velvet drapings, and deep carpeting underfoot. My skirts swished along the dusty floor—and then I stopped.

Could it be? A tiny object on the floor mesmerized me.

A trickle of light fell on the staircase. For a moment I couldn't breathe. On the bottom step something glittered. Against the shadowy backdrop a touch of rainbow light twinkled. I stooped and picked it up. Philippe's amethyst!

The discovery was like a blow to the stomach. I turned it in my hands and then my eyes jerked to the stairs.

Dusty footprints led up the staircase into the black caverns of the deserted hotel.

17

EVERY sensory bud in my body vibrated to pick up the slightest sound that might come to me. My footsteps sounded hollow and terribly loud as I stealthily moved upward from one step to the next. Philippe's amethyst . . . Philippe's amethyst! The phrase played over and over in my mind with the hypnotic chant of a Pied Piper coaxing me into the depths of the hotel.

An obscure, brooding grayness floated down upon me as I reached the first wide landing and moved across it to a flight of steps rising to the second floor. I stopped and peered upward, putting my hand against my throat as if to stifle my own heavy breathing and prevent myself from calling out in mounting terror. A silence like a black abyss waited for one misstep. I shivered. The lacings on my corset seemed to draw tighter as tenseness squeezed like a vise around my middle.

I was afraid. I wanted to run shrieking from the building. Only the stone biting cruelly in my hand as I fiercely clutched it gave me the will to keep going. Dim light spilled onto the stairwell from one high window. I put a trembling hand on a dusty banister and eased upward. My breath came in short gulps as I neared the top, and an invading weakness made me stop.

For the first time I asked myself what I would do if I came upon the kidnapper. My impulsive behavior always ran ahead of rational reasoning. Now I paused. Should I go for help? Where? Who would listen to me? I had failed to find any clue as to where Kipp might be. I was the only one who knew about Philippe taking the amethyst from the ore cabinet. I was certain he had dropped it here, accidentally or on purpose. There was no doubt in my mind that he was somewhere in the hotel. I must find him! Pushing all other thoughts aside, I mounted the top step and cautiously peered both ways down the dusty corridor.

A series of open doors allowed feeble light from windows in the sleeping rooms to filter out into the hall and penetrate the tunnellike darkness. I hesitated, my ears trying to draw in the slightest sound. Settling timbers and noisy wind caught in window cracks mingled with phantom whispers of the deserted building. Which way should I go?

My eyes fell to the floor, searching for the telltale footprints that had led me up from below. I could not believe it! In every direction up and down the hall a layer of dust lay smooth and undisturbed. I blinked. My eyes must be deceiving me!

Where had they gone? Had I been hallucinating? Maybe a trick of light had made me believe I'd seen footprints. No, I refused to accept such malicious trickery. I *had* seen them! Footprints had led up these stairs!

Perhaps I couldn't see them now in the dim, shadow-dappled light, I thought. With my eyes fastened on the floorboards, I walked to my right, to the doorway of the first room. Glancing inside, I saw a barren bedstead, a bowlegged dresser, a commode with washbasin, and an undisturbed, dusty floor. I turned around and looked back the way I had come from the head of the stairs. I could easily see where my long skirts had swept the dirty floor, but in every direction around it, dust lay undisturbed on the hall floor.

Bewildered, with a sense of panic rising, I went back to the head of the stairs and then down the hall in the other direction. When I looked back down the hall, the same pattern: only my skirts had disturbed the dust on the floor. I bit my lip and blinked back tears of frustration. Was I the victim of some taunting, malicious fiend? Then I mentally shook myself. This was no phantasma of my mind. The dusty footprints up the stairs had to go somewhere!

I started down the stairs again, apprehension jangling my taut nerves. The mocking silence taunted me to shout at the top of my lungs to break the stillness. I clamped my mouth shut, moving as stealthily as I could.

At the landing I stopped again, bathed in shards of watery light filtering through the dirty stairwell window. My thoughts thrashed out in every direction. Dusty footprints had led up from the lobby. I had not been mistaken. I refused to think my perceptions had been at fault. No, I had seen them, followed them upward—where had they gone? If the footprints did not go all the way to the top of the stairs . . . ?

At first my mind refused to accept the supposition. I turned slowly around on the gloomy landing. My focus was vague and without direction; then I touched the wainscoted walls and involuntarily gasped a cry of relief. There was the answer. Real and tangible. A small door led off the landing. It was narrow, closed, and had the look of a small closet. It looked so much like the staircase wall that it was no wonder I had missed it. I slowly opened it, not knowing what I expected to see. A closet? A dead body? The barrel of a gun? Then I let out the breath I had been holding. A narrow staircase led upward into darkness. Attic stairs!

I did not hesitate. Holding my skirts close to me, I started up the narrow, steep stairs. Above me a high ceiling vaulted into nothingness. The darkness intensified as I climbed upward, and I wished for a candle. By the time I reached the top, I was blindly feeling my way. My hands touched another closed door and I reached for the knob. By this time I couldn't hear anything but the wild drumming of my own heart.

I held my breath and turned it. As the crack widened, light from a late-afternoon sun shone through dormer windows at the far end of the room. Discarded furniture, trunks, and stacked boxes littered the floor. I had little time to take in the sum total of the perceptions that greeted my senses. A small candle set on a barrel flickered several feet beyond the door. As quietly as I could, I eased toward it. Then my foot struck something soft. I looked down, and a scream exploded in my throat. She lay motionless, a slender woman with eyes staring blindly in death. Fair hair tumbled below her hat, and a torn green veiling swept away from her face. The photograph I had found in the library was suddenly imposed upon her features. A sickening revulsion brought instant recognition. Marianne!

I did not have time to adjust to this appalling discovery of my mystery lady. I sensed another presence . . . but too late!

I turned, catching only the sight of a cane's gold knob as it came crashing down on my skull . . . and then everything was lost in a blinding swirl of unconsciousness that floated me away.

18

THE first sensation that penetrated the blackness was pain. It radiated from the side of my head like red-hot brands slicing and cutting behind my eyes. I groaned silently as my eyelids fluttered open. The view I had was of the floor, boxes, and a man's boots and nankeen trousers as he stood near me.

My mind groped through the pain and dizziness, trying to find my way back to sanity. From one remembered detail I reached for the next, until I remembered where I was. Philippe . . . the hotel . . . the attic . . . Marianne's dead body . . . Kipp's cane descending upon me! This kaleidoscope of horror brought fresh biting pain into my head. My heavy eyelids labored upward. Something bright, inches from my face, wavered and then came into focus. The golden head of Kipp's cane.

I must have cried aloud, but the sound in my ears didn't seem to come from my lips. Fresh pain sliced through my head as I tried to rise. I saw his knees bend and felt large hands upon me. I gasped a cry of protest as my arms were jerked behind me. Rough ropes bit cruelly into my wrists. I struggled against the vicious handling, but I was no match for his strength. Like trussing an animal, he bound me hand and foot.

Kipp . . . Kipp, I sobbed. His betrayal was more than I could stand. As he turned me over, my tortured eyes swept over his face. I gasped. It wasn't Kipp! For an instant my mind could not register the freckled face.

"Chad!"

He nodded soberly. "No harm in your knowing now."

"You!" He was the evil Aunt Esther had written about. Chad—the person I had felt most comfortable with. No, it couldn't be. None of it made sense! His expression left no doubt in my mind that he had killed before . . . and he had little compassion for the pain slicing my arms and legs. "But why . . . why?" I croaked. This stammering was all I could manage aloud. Inside my mind the questions were darting spears. "Why did you do it? What do you want?"

He gave a short laugh. "You are so stupid, Allison. At first I was afraid that you might put things together, that's why I tried to get you out of the way the second day you were here—on the cliff."

"You . . . you pushed me! But why? Why?"

"The hotel. I tried to make your aunt sell it, but she turned to Kipp instead and gave him half-interest in it. Then you showed up, and that put three of you in the way of my ever getting it cheap."

"Why would you kill for it? The hotel isn't worth anything!"

He gave a mirthless laugh. "That's what everybody thinks, but I know different. Your uncle stumbled onto its worth, and that's why I had to get him out of the way quick. I was helping him with the remodeling, putting up timbers and digging out the wine cellar. We carried out dirt and rock to the ravine—then we discovered gold specks in some of the rocks. A strong clear vein!"

"Gold," I breathed. *The hotel was sitting on a rich vein of gold!*

"I see you've got the picture," he said, watching my face. "I hit your uncle over the head with a rock and sent him over the edge. All work on the hotel stopped, and I made sure that business fell off so badly that there was no money left to finish the wine cellar. My secret was safe."

"You arranged all those malicious happenings! And you assaulted my aunt!"

"The stubborn old woman gave me no choice. I couldn't wait around for her to stumble on to the fact that she was literally sitting on a gold mine! I figured if she were out of the way, the hotel would be put up for sale. But you had to arrive on the scene!"

"You pushed me over the cliff and drugged my cider!"

"I had to make certain that you didn't decide to follow in your dear aunt's footsteps and keep the hotel. You brought all this on yourself, Allison. Now it's done. Halstead's out of the picture. His share of the hotel will be sold. That smelter explosion wiped him out."

"But you were there when it happened. I saw you . . . with the doctor. How did you . . .?"

"Easy," he bragged. "I waited until Kipp had gone, then set the charge of dynamite. Then I went out and rolled in the dirt behind an ore car and let her blow! I knew he had every cent invested in that smelter. He's flat busted!" His grin was sadistic. "He had to borrow on his house and everything he owns to pay the ransom . . . and that's what I'll use to buy the hotel. Smart, eh? Time my luck changed. I'll be the important fellow in these parts now."

I moistened my lips. "Where is Kipp?"

"Doing some digging of his own . . . and not for gold." His laugh was boisterous. "I met him at the Old Nellie mine, ambushed him, and collected the ransom. I left him unconscious in the tunnel . . . set a small charge of dynamite at the entrance. Closed it up nice, it did. Those rotten timbers were ready to give way."

I mustn't faint, I told myself. Hold on. In the face of this madness there had to be something I could do. I must keep him talking. "How could you?"

"Why not? He took my claim from me."

"He bought it from you!"

"Sure . . . after I put my guts into working it! He had money when I didn't. Well, now I've got money!" He sobered. "I was afraid he wouldn't come through for the boy. I was glad when you told me yesterday that he would."

That was it! The avarice in Chad's eyes when we were talking about the ransom. I had sensed it, but wrongly identified it as concern. And now it was too late. Kipp had paid the ransom and had been left sealed up in a mine.

"And Philippe?" I voiced the name in a near-whisper.

"Over there on the bed. Gave him some laudanum, so he's been sleeping."

Thank God, he was alive. "You took him from the house after you killed my aunt?"

"No, Marianne did that. She still had keys to the house, so she let us in. Your aunt was wandering around the hall, so I took care of her in the parlor while Marianne got the boy. She brought him here while I played the good friend and made certain Kipp raised the money for my ransom note."

"But why did you kill Marianne . . . if she helped you?"

"I have to have all the ransom money so I can buy the hotel. Marianne was nothing but a cheap gold digger anyway. She came back to Glen Eyrie to shake Kipp down for some more money. Then she found out he was strapped for funds— that he didn't have any ready cash for her greedy hands."

"Did . . . did he know she was in Glen Eyrie?" I had to know.

"Naw. She kept out of sight, trying to figure out what was the best way to shake him down. Millie hid her out—sisters under the skin, so to speak. Marianne promised to cut her in on whatever she could get from Kipp, so Millie lied to him when he came asking about a veiled woman who had come up on the train with you."

"Then she was in the carriage with Millie's new boarder . . . and at the cabin . . . and on the bridle path!"

"Yep. She insisted on keeping her eye on you two. Anyway, I talked her into the ransom idea and helping me get rid of you. She was more than willing, by the way, seeing the way things were going between you and Halstead. Nothing so cooperative as a jealous woman." He gave a dirty laugh. "She'd been using Philippe against you, until the boy decided he could trust you more than his mother and refused to cooperate after that first time when he did as Marianne told him."

"She was the one poisoning his mind against me."

"That's right, and I was waiting on the cliff when you came out at the spot we had arranged. Who would have thought a miracle would save you? Every time, the fates intervened . . . but now you've walked right into my loving hands."

"I thought you were my friend," I said angrily. "I never once suspected it might be you. What about your conscience?" I knew it was useless to appeal to him on this level, but I had to try. For the moment I was filled with fury that he had duped me so completely.

"I guess the parson's right. The devil calls his own. Churchgoing never did me no good. I've already taken four lives, Marianne's, Halstead's and the Laceys. Same amount of hell for two more, I reckon."

"Please, please, Chad . . . let us go."

"Don't be pleading with me like that. I'm not fooled by it. You're Halstead's bitch now." His freckles stood out angrily on his face like pox. "There's only one thing left to do. Burn down the hotel. Then I can buy the land cheap and file a claim for the gold." He roughly jerked me up and carried me across the room to a bed like those I had seen in the deserted rooms downstairs. In the middle of a bare mattress was a small boy. Philippe's eyes were open and his little body tugged at his ropes as Chad laid me down beside him.

I managed a feeble smile and was rewarded by a flash of joy in those deep-set eyes. He looked so small and vulnerable that anger warmed my chilled body. I turned on Chad. "You can't do this . . . not to an innocent child!"

"Won't do no good to be yelling your guts out," answered Chad shortly, ignoring my angry plea. "Nobody comes near this hotel anymore, not after I got through playing my tricks and making everyone think it was a bad-luck place." He chuckled. "Well, everything turns out for the best, I guess. It's still your hotel I'll be burning down, yours and Halstead's . . . and in my book you both deserve everything you get."

"But not the boy," I pleaded. "Let Philippe go. He hasn't done you any harm."

"But he would talk." Chad looped another

rope through my bound feet and tied them to the bedpost in the same fashion he had secured Philippe.

"He'd keep quiet. Besides, who would believe a little boy?" I pleaded.

"Everybody. He's Kipp Halstead's son—how long do you think it'd be before they caught up with me and strung a noose around my neck?"

"But if . . . if you set fire to this building, you could burn down the whole town."

He scoffed. "This place is set off by itself. Just be a nice little bonfire . . . and no harm done."

No harm done!

He swung around and was gone. His footsteps made a haunting thump as he left the attic.

I jerked at my bonds as if by some mysterious fashion they would dissolve and I would be free to grab Philippe and flee. Pain lashed through my legs. The hands tied behind me pulsated with a fiery ache.

"He ties tough knots," said Philippe weakly, as if he had already struggled against his in the same fashion.

His pathetic little voice settled my rising hysteria. I bit back sobs rising in my throat. "Yes, I'm afraid he does." I moved my head as close to the child as I could, and he reponded by inching toward me until we were cheek to cheek.

"Are you all right? They didn't hurt you?"

"He's a bad man."

"Yes, he is."

"He did something bad to my mother, didn't he?"

Dear God, give me the right words, I thought in despair. How could I hope to make sense of all this to a bewildered little boy?

He must have sensed my struggle, for he didn't wait for me to answer. "I heard what he said. He killed her. My mom just wanted money . . . she didn't want me."

"But your father wants you . . . and I want you, Philippe. We've been terribly worried about you . . . looking everywhere."

"Not my father. He'd be glad I was gone," he countered in his usual pugnacious tone.

"You're wrong. Your father is terribly worried. And, Philippe, he paid a lot of money to get you back. It cost him about everything he owns to raise that money. He paid it because he loves you. No matter what happens, you have to know that. Your father loves you." My voice broke.

"Then why didn't he come . . . instead of you?" His voice was still belligerent. "I dropped my amethyst so he would find it."

"Your father was told to take the ransom money to the Old Nellie mine, but Chad ambushed him—took the money and left him there . . . unconscious." I closed my eyes as if to lessen the pain of those words. Kipp. Forgive me, Kipp, for ever doubting you. Both Philippe and I had been wrong about him. "Don't you see, he put his own life in danger for you. Chad must have overpowered him, taken his cane, and closed up the tunnel."

"Can't he get out?"

"Chad said he sealed up the entrance."

"He's not dead, is he?"

I blinked back tears and tried to keep my voice even. "I don't know. If someone gets to him soon enough . . ." My voice trailed off.

"Like you got to me?" he asked innocently. "I dropped my stone on purpose."

"That was a very smart thing to do. I saw it and knew you were here. I just wish . . ." My voice trailed off. If only I had told Tooley or Mary or someone where I was going. Chad was downstairs setting a fire. There wasn't any time. In a few minutes the whole building would go up like a torch. I had to do something—but what? Both of us were bound hand and foot and tied to the bedstead. The only thing Chad hadn't done was gag us. But it was true—no one would hear our shouts. No one came near the hotel anymore. No one but Kipp . . . and he couldn't help us now. New fear belted me. If someone didn't get to him soon, he would be suffocated in an abandoned mine. No one would know he was there. I was the only one who might save him!

My frantic gaze went around the room. Nothing I could see would help. Besides, everything was out of reach. There were a jug of water and the remains of a sandwich where Marianne must have eaten while waiting for Chad to come back with the ransom money. Instead he had buried it in his old diggings and come back and killed her. If I hadn't surprised him, he would have already set the fire . . . and Philippe would never have been found.

There were only a few minutes left.

Think . . . think!

I couldn't see any way to get loose. The ropes were strong and firmly tied. Already my hands and feet were numb. Struggling only seemed to shut off more circulation. My impulse was to scream. If I had been alone, I might have given in to pure hysterics, but the small boy at my side made me struggle for control—and pray for a miracle. The minutes ticked off in frightening certainty. There wasn't going to be any miracle. Hot tears eased into my eyes. I had never been one to give in easily, and this helpless, lost, and defeated feeling drowned my last flicker of hope.

"I'm hungry," Philippe said, breaking into my whirlwind thoughts as if we had all the time in the world for such creature comforts. All those meals when Tooley had struggled to put food in his mouth—and now he was asking to eat. Condemned men always got a last meal, I thought incoherently.

Eat!

A thought whirled in my brain like a cue. I chased it around. What was the elusive connotation about eating that was escaping me? *Come on . . . think! Think!* What was the connection between the word "eat" and a spurt of knowledge that lay just beyond my grasp?

Eat . . . chew? That was it! Chew!

I swallowed to get some moisture into my dry mouth. I turned my head, facing Philippe. "Honey, do you think you could scoot around so that I could get my mouth at the knots holding your hands?" I tried to keep my voice light and encouraging. "That's it . . . turn . . . and put your back toward me . . . that's it . . . now move up in bed . . . no, I can't reach you." I stretched my neck as far as it would go. "A little farther."

"I can't. It hurts."

"I know . . . but, please, Philippe, curl up and stretch your arms back as far as they will go. Please try." I wanted to scream at him that a few minutes lay between us and death. "Now, try again . . . good!"

I twisted and bent and stretched and finally nuzzled my teeth between those tiny hands and wrists. I opened my mouth and found the raised knot. Like a rodent, I set my teeth upon it. If only I could grasp one of the strands, it might loosen . . . or tighten! I pulled back. The knot did not give. If anything, it seemed to tighten.

"It hurts," wailed Philippe.

"I'm sorry . . . don't move . . . lie still . . . I'm going to untie the knot with my teeth." I said it as if there were no question about the success of my biting and pulling and searching for the one end that would loosen and come free.

As one part of my brain worked like a frantic creature chewing and tugging at the fibers, a sense of urgency collected sobs in my throat. Time was running out! My anxiety must have communicated itself to the boy, for he said in a muffled voice, "Can't you hurry, Allie?"

Allie! I almost cried, the pain and joy were so intense. Then I bit at the knot again . . . and again, tugging . . . pulling . . . biting. Was it coming loose? Was I making progress at all! Tears flooded my eyes. When the knot finally gave, I thought it was my imagination. I pulled back on a strand—and it slipped out of the square knot.

"You did it!" squeaked Philippe as his little hands slipped out of the rope. The rest came quickly, and in another minute Philippe had wriggled free. He squealed and held his hands up for me to see!

I gave a shaky laugh and then my nostrils sent a terrifying message. Smoke! I smelled smoke! *Chad had set the hotel on fire!*

"Philippe, listen!" My voice was strident. "Undo the knots on your feet. Right now! Quick!"

His little fingers fumbled at the tight knot.

"Hurry . . . that's it . . . no, pull on the other one . . . it's giving way . . . pull harder . . . now slip that end out of the other. Good! *Thank God! He was free!* Now run downstairs and out the door . . . and down to the livery stable. Stay there until someone comes for you. Now, go!"

"I'll untie you, Allie."

"There isn't time to work the knots. Go! Run!"

"For help?"

"Yes, for help," I lied, for I knew how fast the building would burn and collapse, but he wasn't going to go without this encouragement. "Go for help!"

Like a shot he was across the room and I heard his flying footsteps down the stairs. Then his strangled cough floated up the narrow staircase and I knew he had run into smoke.

Had the flames already reached the landing? *Please, God, let him get out . . . please keep him safe.* What if he never made it to the outside door . . . what if Chad lurked outside watching his handiwork . . . what if . . .? Stop it! The boy had a chance . . . she had given him a chance. *Please, Philippe . . . get away . . . get away!*

19

AN acrid, biting smoke eased through the floor-boards as a thickening gray haze began to fill the attic room. My mouth and throat were instantly parched with an invading dryness. From somewhere on the floors below a faint crackling of licking flames greeted my ears. Kipp's office? I visualized that beautiful English desk and Kipp's personal things feeding a greedy, quickly spreading fire. Yes, it would appeal to Chad's vengeful hatred to start the fire there.

How could I have been so blind? My own jealousy had settled my suspicions upon Lucretia. Her abrasive, mercenary attitude made me identify her as the villain, while Chad's friendly freckled face had lulled me into accepting him as a hometown boy instead of a disillusioned gold seeker who would do anything to get his hands on a rich strike. When he saw the gold-laced ore in my uncle's hands he had reacted to a diabolical greed that set him upon a murderous path. He ruined my aunt's business so he could get his hands on the hotel, but Kipp had intervened, lending her money, and finally becoming part-owner. Lucretia had been right: it was Kipp's involvement with my aunt's affairs that had brought bad luck rushing upon him, wiping out his financial resources. Kipp! My lover had given up everything for me and my family. How could I bear to think of him buried inside a mountain, maybe already dead . . . or suffocating to death? Sobs rose and fell in my chest. I closed my eyes tightly, trying not to think about the inferno growing and spreading on the floor below me. At least Philippe—

The rest of that thought was cut off. It couldn't be. A light bounding of feet up the attic staircase stabbed me with recognition.

No, Philippe, no! *The child was coming back!*

A spasm of coughing came closer. In another minute Philippe was beside the bed. "Too smoky," he said in that belligerent tone, his eyes watering and his chest heaving with coughs. His dark hair and petite features were hazy in the thickening smoke.

Dear God in heaven! I could have paddled him good!

"Now, listen to me!" My no-nonsense tone was that of a schoolmistress to a truculent pupil. "Take out the hankie you'll find in my pocket . . . get it, Philippe! Now!"

His little hand fumbled in the jacket pocket of my riding habit. "Good!" I said when he had the lace handkerchief in his hand. It was one that one of my students had hemstitched for me. Who would have thought it would be used in such dire straits as this? "Now, wet it in that jug of water . . . and then pour the rest of the water over your clothes. Hold the cloth over your nose and mouth and run downstairs and outside. Now! Philippe . . . now!''

''But—''

''Go! Don't argue! Do as I say.'' A spasm of coughing overtook me. The membranes in my nose and throat were trying to refuse the invading smoke. Through smarting eyes I saw him turn away from the bed. Thank God. Tears coated my face. Hurry! Hurry! Hurry!

I let my head fall back on the bed. Desperately I struggled against my bonds again, knowing the frantic gestures only made the rope burn deeper into my flesh. Sobs caught in my throat. The dry boards and dusty furnishings would feed the fire at a rapid rate. There was so a little time left. If he didn't get through the lobby before it was engulfed in flames, he wouldn't be able to get out at all! I squinted into the swirling, thick haze. I couldn't see him anymore. Had he gone? Had he used the water as I instructed.

''Philippe?''

No answer.

I let out a strangled sigh of relief. Then my eyes flew open. He was at the side of the bed again!

''Look what I found. A knife.'' His childish voice bubbled excitedly as he held out an old hunting knife.

''Philippe! There's no time!'' I wanted to shake those stubborn little shoulders. ''Find the water and wet the hankie.''

He shook his head willfully. "I'll cut you loose first." His father's determined tone threaded his boyish voice, and I knew it was useless to protest. If only there were more time. Was the attic staircase already in flames?

"Tooley taught me how to gut fish," Philippe said proudly, as if that qualified him to handle the long blade that hung heavily in his hand.

There was no time left to argue. He wasn't going to leave. Somehow I had to get loose and take him out. "All right." I twisted as much as possible, lying with my back to him. "Hurry . . . hurry!"

I winced as I felt the sharp end of the knife pierce my wrists. He must have drawn blood, for he gasped and pulled the blade away.

"It's all right," I soothed, stilling an urge to scream hysterically. "Put the knife on top of the knot and saw back and forth. Don't worry about blood. It doesn't hurt. Hurry, Philippe."

Once more I felt the stab of the knife. The blade was too thick and long for him to use efficiently. Back and forth . . . back and forth. Endless motion . . . and without results. The blade was probably dull and rusty. No telling how long it had been lying around the attic. "Is it cutting the rope?" I asked as the seconds stretched to an agonizing eternity.

"A little bit."

"Good. Can you go a little faster?" I coaxed, trying to keep the panic out of my voice. The drug he had been given was undoubtedly slowing his reactions. His valiant effort to cut the thick rope demanded more physical strength than he had. If only he had gone when there was a chance!

I stifled a cry as he stabbed me viciously again with the point of the knife.

Hurry . . . hurry!

He was coughing harder now. My nostrils recoiled from the stench of burning wood and cloth and I could hear the crackling sounds of a fire. Frantically I pulled against the cords as hard as I could—and I felt a strand snap!

Philippe gave a childish cry of delight. He was sawing faster now. Another piece of the cord snapped. The knot gave enough so I could slip one hand out . . . and then the other. My hands were free!

I gave a strangled sob and sat up. My fingers fumbled at the rope holding my feet to the bedstead. With some concerted effort it miraculously fell away. Philippe gave a childish laugh. "I did it!"

"Bring me the water jug," I croaked. "Carefully . . . don't drop it!"

I stood up and quickly loosened the drawstring on my petticoat. I kicked it up into my hands and tore it in two as best I could. Then with the knife I jabbed two holes in one piece, wet it, and put it over Philippe's head. Thank God Marianne had brought water with her up to the attic. "We're going to play ghost," I said reassuringly. I could hear his childish giggle as his eyes peered through the holes at me. The horror of the moment still evaded him. He was not aware that we were minutes away from a horrible death of suffocation or searing flames.

With a calm that defied the screaming hysterics battering my insides, I poured water on the other cloth, jabbed two holes, and put it over my own head. I splashed the remaining water over our clothes. It was a feeble gesture and I knew the cloth would undoubtedly be dry before we left the attic.

I grabbed Philippe's hand and we dashed across the attic and darted downward in the smoke-filled passage. I pulled him so fast down the steps that his feet barely hit wood. *If only Chad had started the fire in Kipp's office, the front staircase might not yet be in flames.*

We stumbled out onto the landing. My heart sank. Tongues of orange flame were coming up the stairway from an inferno raging in the lobby.

There was no place to go but up! The whole staircase would be in flames shortly. Heat blistered my eyes through the holes of my torn petticoat, and our clothes were drying out like a washing set beside a fire. A few moments more and all dampness would have left the torn petticoat protecting our faces. My lungs filled with the biting, pungent odor of burning wood and cloth.

At the top of the stairs I hesitated. Most of the hotels and boardinghouses had a flight of steep steps going up the sides of the building. If only there were such a door at the end of this hall!

"I can't see . . . I can't see!" Philippe's muffled cry came from under the hood. He pulled back like a young mule setting his heels. His hand came up and he jerked off the wet cloth.

"Leave that on!" I gasped, but he had already thrown it away and it was lost in the swirling smoke rising like a black mist around us.

I picked him up in my arms and pressed his face against my chest, wavering unsteadily with the weight that ordinarily would have been impossible to handle.

A hideous orange glow lit up the inside of the building. I could see dancing flames leaping from the floor below like fiendish specters outside the bedroom windows. If the fire reached the roof, I realized with a new thrust of panic, the whole building could collapse!

I stumbled forward. I could not see ahead because of the smoke and the cloth over my head, which cut off my peripheral vision. Philippe clutched my neck with a scissors hold and he buried his face against me like a baby snuggling into the warmth of his mother's shoulder. He whimpered softly.

My strength ebbed in a spasm of coughing that tore at my insides. Oxygen in the thin air was being burned up at an alarming rate. My lungs burned as I opened my mouth and gasped against the rapidly drying cloth. I knew that our only chance lay in finding an outside door at the end of this second-floor hall. I prayed one would be there!

As a swirling black haze engulfed me, I weaved drunkenly from side to side. Sometimes losing my balance, I scraped against the side walls of the hall. My body protested the loss of oxygen to my limbs as muscles began to cramp. I willed my legs to take one step . . . and then another. With my head bent forward, blindly I labored forward with my heavy burden. Suddenly a blow on my head nearly sent me to my knees. I had run into the wall at the end of the corridor.

I set Philippe down, holding him firmly with one hand and searching the wall like a blind man with the other. If there was an outside door, it would be here. My hand scraped over the wood as I tried to focus through smarting, tearful eyes to find some hint of a doorjamb.

Philippe was crying now, emitting deep, coughing wails. He screamed pitifully as a thundering crash in the depths of the building reached our ears. There was no place to go now! We were trapped at the end of the hall. Our clothes were dry and the thickening smoke invaded our lungs. I wanted to fall to my knees and hold him in my arms these last minutes. Some stubborn willfulness would not let me surrender. I pounded both hands on the wood as if anguish alone would create an escape from the fiery trap.

Philippe clutched my legs as he cowered beside me. A frantic sweep of my hand touched something to my right. Metal? I forced a deliberate slow motion back again. Where was it? Had I been mistaken? Was I hallucinating because I couldn't face reality?

No. There it was, under my fingers. Narrow and grooved. A door hinge! I had missed the door by only a few inches. If I'd given up, we would have slumped unconscious to the floor a few steps from safety.

I felt my way across the door panel and found the doorknob . . . turned it.

Locked!

Defeat claimed me then. With one hand still holding on to Philippe, I leaned my head against the door and a convulsive sob shook my body. Hysterically I banged on the wood-panels. Crying. Sobbing. Coughing. Strength ebbed away. In one wild, frantic flailing of my one free hand I touched something hard.

What? My hands fastened on it.

An iron bolt!

With a muffled cry of recognition I pulled at it. Miraculously, it slid easily in its casing. A spurt of new strength brought my hand back to the doorknob. It opened!

Air rushed in—blessed, clear, wonderful air! Sobbing, I pulled Philippe out on a wooden landing. Blinking against the swirling clouds of smoke, I saw a narrow staircase clinging precariously to the side of the building. Miraculously, no flames licked at our feet. The fire had not reached this side of the hotel. We were safe!

Gasping the life-giving air, we stumbled down the stairs.

We had made it! We had made it!

Then Philippe gave a horrifying shriek and pointed.

I jerked my head around.

Coming out of the trees, where he had been watching the torched building, Chad lunged toward us at a dead run, swearing. His face was flushed with anger. His fists were clenched, and I knew he was prepared to crush us with his bare hands.

I screamed as he reached us. My hands flayed his face, but I was no match for the steel-strong arms that went around Philippe and me. Like a hunter bringing in game, Chad dragged us away from the burning building into the nearby copse of dark conifers.

It was twilight now. The sun had abandoned the valley to the dull gray of that time of evening between sun and moonlight. The burning building glowed a brassy orange and red as clouds of rolling smoke rose like black thunderheads.

Some part of my consciousness registered the clang of a fire bell in the distance. Someone was coming! But even as the thought brought a surge of hope, I knew it was too late. We were already out of sight of the hotel in the thick band of trees behind it.

I knew then what Chad intended to do. He had already killed once on that rocky precipice behind the hotel where he and my uncle had dumped the rocks from the wine cellar. I twisted and writhed, but his arm was like an iron vise around my middle. My seared lungs were still burning from the smoke inhalation I had endured in the hotel. I feared that Philippe was nearly unconscious, for even his whimpering had faded away. He dangled from Chad's other arm like a broken marionette.

"You bitch," he swore as my nails raked at his face. "How in the hell did you get loose? Good thing I hung around to make sure of the job! Couldn't believe my eyes when I saw you coming out that door."

"Please . . . please, let the boy go."

He gave a short laugh. "Sure I will. Let him go and have a posse on me by nightfall. No . . . it has to be another accident . . . another unfortunate fall over the cliff."

"You can't—"

"Who's going to stop me? Everyone knows you don't have any sense about wandering around these mountains. They'll think you took the boy with you." He gave a horrible chuckle. "It all fits. You're the kidnapper! You tried to blackmail Halstead but missed your footing trying to hide out with the boy. You could have even set the dynamite that sealed up the mine with him in it."

"No one would believe that," I protested with what little breath I had left.

"Sure they would. Lucretia's ready to believe the worst about you. Yep, this way is better all around. Thanks for tying up all the loose ends for me." He then dropped Philippe on the ground, and the small body lay quiet in a crumpled heap. I wondered if Chad had squeezed the breath out of him. "I'll take care of him in a minute. You first."

We were on the lip of a deep gulch. Chad stooped to pick up a rock. With the last reserve of my strength I twisted out of his grasp. I took a staggering step . . . and then he had me again!

He swore, raised his arm. I saw the rock clutched in his hand. With a cry, I cowered, trying to protect my head.

I waited, but the vicious blow never came.

As I prepared for the crashing burst of pain in my skull, his tight grip on my waist slackened. It took me a moment to react. My eyes flew open. Through squinting, blurry vision I saw Kipp astride Midnight. He had grabbed Chad's arm at the last second as it was raised to bash in my skull. *He had escaped from the mine!* His face was blackened, his clothes dirty and disheveled as he flung himself from the saddle. Chad lunged at him, and the next instant the two men were locked in mortal combat.

I could tell that Kipp was weary, for his reactions were slow, but his tenacity kept him coming at Chad again and again. I screamed as they rolled dangerously near the edge, one lunging at the other, swinging and punching until I wondered how either had the strength left to stand.

Philippe had regained the breath Chad had squeezed out of him, and he rushed into my arms, crying brokenly. I wanted to run for help, but I was riveted to the spot. It was a nightmare, and the horror of it froze me as I held Philippe and watched Kipp spin from a blow. Chad rushed at him.

I screamed as flying arms and legs went over the side of the cliff. Somehow Kipp had recovered his footing, and it was Chad's cry that ended in a deadening thud at the bottom of the gulch.

I sobbed hysterically as he gathered both Philippe and me into his arms. "Thank God I dug out in time," he said in a tremulous voice.

"How . . . how did you do it?"

"Found an old pick and shovel in the tunnel. There was a thin spot in the rockfall, and I dug through. I've been at it for hours."

"But how did you know to come here?" I still couldn't believe he had appeared at the critical moment.

"Chad told me he and Marianne had taken Philippe to the hotel. I honestly didn't know she was here, Allie."

"I know you didn't. It's all right. Everything's going to be fine."

Crying and laughing and hugging, the three of us shared the wonderment of being alive . . . and together . . . and unharmed.

Then Philippe looked up at both of us, his eyes soft and shiny. He put one hand in mine and the other in his father's, and pulling at us, he said, "Let's go home now."

20

OUR new home was built on the emerald meadow behind Kipp's cabin. It was a rambling, spacious house, warm with natural woods, large windows, and open spaces which harmonized with the mountain panorama beyond its doors. Its homey rooms were filled with the lovely furnishings Kipp had brought from his family home, and they found new beauty in these surroundings. The gentle meadow cupped by aspen and conifer forests was our front yard. A swift-flowing stream played through the alpine glen and formed a small pool which became our private miniature lake. Kipp and I took long rides through the forests to picnic by a foaming cataract of some high mountain waterfall, and I waded through creeks collecting rocks and polliwogs with Philippe. Eagles spread their wings, soaring in floating circles above the house and nesting in the nearby ridges, but they no longer frightened me. All dark shadows had fallen away and my spirits were free to soar in harmony with them.

The rich tapestry of my life was in sharp contrast to the sterile life at Miss Purcell's finishing school. When I wrote to the dear lady that I was going to be married, her response was both congratulatory and concerned. She sent me a small volume about marriage that was supposed to help an innocent young woman respond to her husband's wishes. I giggled. I had never been that innocent, I mused, remembering how I had responded from the first moment to Kipp's embrace.

I wished she could have been at our wedding in the small church. The day was gloriously clear and wonderful, with soft clouds like clotted cream moving lazily against the periwinkle blue of the sky. Happy is the bride the sun shines on, I thought.

Kipp's eyes reflected a teasing and appreciative smile as I came down the aisle toward him. My bridal gown was more beautiful than the *Delineator* pattern had promised. Ellie Peters, the seamstress, had fashioned with painstaking stiches a white satin bodice with a deep inset of lace running from the high neck to a point on the waist, a full veil and train trimmed with matching Urling lace. We chose scattered pearls to decorate santag sleeves whose puffs were held in place by pearl bands. A tiara of silver sat high on my blond-red tresses, their soft wisps of curls lightly framing my face. Ellie Peters' squinty eyes grew moist as I passed her.

I could see Philippe's small head as he sat in the front row. He was losing more of his shell every day and developing into a high-spirited, lovable little boy. I heard his high-pitched giggle as he whispered excitedly to Tooley—and his Mary. True to his word, the Irishman had not taken a drink since Philippe's safe return. He had no need for drink to wipe out the anguish of the past, for Mary had agreed to become his wife. They would be married soon and live in a house being built near ours.

On the opposite side of the aisle I glimpsed a straight back, long neck, and austere profile. Lucretia! I knew that I had wronged her by thinking she had been responsible for all the treachery, but I was certain of one thing: she was not rejoicing that her efforts to separate me from Kipp had failed. This wedding was not to her liking. Perhaps in time she would accept me, but I knew we would never be friends. She had secured the house she wanted . . . but not the master. She was welcome to the unfriendly house. I never looked up at it perched high on the bluff without remembering its cold, brooding aura.

As I reached the altar where Reverend Gilly stood with his Bible in hand, I raised my gaze to Kipp's handsome face and delighted at the deep love I saw there. His elegant attire was that of an aristocratic gentleman, formal black coat, striped trousers, white ruffled shirt, and black tie knotted under a stiff collar. The ripple of muscles that lay under the smooth attire was familiar to me and I had felt the long, sweet length of his legs against mine. This remembered intimacy brought a warm pink flush to my cheeks that must have been seen through my wedding veil.

One of his gray-blue eyes lowered in a roguish wink. His mouth curved silently, to form the words "I love you." I smiled back my answer as we turned to face the preacher.

In the high, glorious splendor of the Rockies, the words of the service were a benediction to a commitment we had already made.

Lee Karr, a native of Colorado, resides in Denver. The nearby Rocky Mountains were the background for her two other romantic suspense novels, *The Housesitter* and *Tangled Mesh*. While raising four children with her husband, Marshall, and pursuing a career as a reading specialist, she has written articles and short stories for regional and professional magazines and co-authored "A Design For Individualized Reading." She was honored by the International Reading Association as one of Colorado's Outstanding Teachers.